CHANTEL NUNN

Whispers Of The Dead

Acknowledgments

Trigger Warning / Content Note

This book contains material that may be distressing or triggering to some readers.

Whispers of the Dead includes graphic depictions and references to:

- Sexual assault (past and referenced, including trafficking)
- Physical, psychological, and emotional abuse
- Obsessive and coercive relationships
- Violence (including murder, torture, and graphic injury)
- Self-harm and suicidal ideation
- Pregnancy complications and threats to mother/child
- Death of loved ones, including on-page grief and trauma
- Gaslighting, manipulation, and captivity
- Stalking and threats
- Mental health struggles (PTSD, panic attacks, dissociation, flashbacks)
- Substance use (alcohol, implied prescription meds)

This is a **pitch-black dark romance** intended for mature readers (18+).

Please prioritize your wellbeing and do not continue if any of these topics are harmful to your mental health.

For resources or support, consider reaching out to a mental health professional or support line.

One

Chapter 1

Sophia's laughter filled the room. For a moment, it was the way Amelia remembered her. Bright and reckless. Sophia's hand reached for hers across the bed, warm and familiar. Amelia almost smiled. Then the warmth turned wet and sticky.

Sophia's fingers slipped in her grip, coated in blood. The laugh fractured into a choking gasp. Her throat was slit open, purple and raw. Her eyes, once alive, now rolled glassy and accusing.

You should have saved me.

The words weren't spoken, they carved themselves into Amelia's bones. Her body wouldn't move. All she could do was watch as Sophia reached again, her bruised hand clawing through the dark and dragging her down into it.

Blood pooled on the floorboards, creeping higher. Sophia's face dipped, eyes wide and mouth trying to form the words

Amelia couldn't bear to hear.

You let me die.

Then the laugh came again. Sharp and broken. The sound followed her, clinging like hands around her throat. For a split second she couldn't tell if her eyes were open or if the darkness was still the dream's. The weight of Sophia's stare pressed against her ribs, squeezing.

Amelia sat up, gasping. The air thick and tight in her lungs. Her heart hammered so hard she thought it might burst through her ribs. Sweat slicked her hair to her forehead, clinging to her like a second skin. She shivered violently, every muscle coiled and trembled. Her sheets were twisted around her legs, damp. She clawed at them, trying to pull herself free.

Her chest heaved, breath ragged, fingers digging into the mattress as if holding on would stop the world from spinning. Her stomach knotted, nausea curling through her, and a cold tremor ran down her spine. She pressed a trembling hand to her sternum, trying to ground herself, but her limbs felt weak.

It had been three weeks since Ethan vanished. Three weeks since blood spilled across the floor and everyone swore no man could crawl away from. But Amelia knew better. Monsters like him didn't die. They rotted and they waited.

She slid free from Lucas's hold and walked over to the window. The glass rattled faintly in its frame, rain painting the street.

Her reflection wavered back at her, only it wasn't her own.

Sophia stood in the glass. Her head tilted and lips curved almost like a smile. But her eyes were hollow and endless.

Amelia's throat closed and her nails bit into the window

ledge. She blinked and then Sophia was gone.

By morning, she told herself it was nothing. Just a dream leaking into daylight.

Lucas paced the kitchen like a predator in a cage, jaw tight enough to see the muscle twitch at his temple. He slammed the mug down; coffee spilled, steaming over his hand, but he barely flinched. His eyes, dark and sharp, scanned the room, flickering to every corner, every shadow.

"He's still out there," he muttered, low and dangerous. His fingers twitched at his side, clenching and unclenching as if itching for a weapon. For a split second, he paused by the window, gaze hard, jaw slackening just a touch as worry flickered beneath the fury.

"He won't stop," Lucas said, his voice flat. "Not until he's buried."

She pulled the blanket tighter around her shoulders, throat closing. "Then we bury him."

The silence that followed was heavy, thick enough to choke on.

Lucas stood by the window, eyes scanning the street like he expected Ethan's shadow to crawl out of it. Amelia sat at the table, picking at the edge of the blanket, neither of them speaking. The minutes dragged, stretched thin until they felt sharp.

By noon, the silence shattered. A knock hammered against the front door. Lucas moved like a wire snapping, the knife in hand. He yanked the door open, ready for blood.

But it wasn't Ethan. It was a girl.

She was barefoot and soaked through. Her lip split and her

hair plastered to her face. She swayed once then crumbled forward into Amelia's arms.

Her breath came in sharp rattles. Blood smeared across Amelia's shirt, warm and wet. Her fingers clawed at her, like she was drowning.

"He said…" Her voice shook. "He said he'd came back. That you'd never be free."

And then it hit her, a scent. Sweet, impossibly familiar. Her stomach lurched. She was wearing Sophia's perfume.

It wrapped around her like a ghost, heavy and clinging, dredging up memory after memory she wasn't ready to face. Her head swam, her chest tightening as if the air had been stolen from her lungs. For one fleeting and torturous moment, she almost believed Sophia was there, laughing and reaching for her hand. The scent overwhelmed her senses.

The girl's body went limp and in the silence that followed, Amelia swore she heard Sophia laugh.

Lucas checked the girl's pulse. "She's alive," he said. "Barely."

Amelia's arms were locked around the girl's limp body. She could feel every bone pressing through the skin.

Lucas hauled the girl from her and laid her out on the floor. His hands moved fast, checking her breathing and tilting her head back. The girl coughed, blood flecking her lips.

"She's been through hell," Lucas said. His voice flat but his eyes burned with rage. "This is Ethan's work."

The name felt like a knife dragged slow across Amelia's skin. Her gaze dropped to the girl in front of her. For a second, she wasn't looking at a stranger. She was looking at Sophia. Pale, broken and gone. The scent of the perfume hung in the air, sweet and impossible to ignore. It surrounded Amelia and made her feel dizzy.

Her breath stuttered and she pressed her palm hard against the floor, just to feel something solid.

Lucas's voice cut through. "Amelia, look at me."

She dragged her eyes up to him. "She's not Sophia," he said, as if he could read the thoughts that were swirling around in her head. "Don't go there."

But Amelia couldn't stop. The image wouldn't fade. Sophia's hands in hers, her laugh echoing around her.

Her chest tightened until she thought her ribs might snap. Outside thunder broke. The walls shuddered like the house itself was bracing for something far worse.

Two

Chapter 2

The girl coughed and her eyes cracked open, wild and unfo-cused, darting from Amelia and Lucas like she couldn't tell if either of them were real.

Her lips trembled. "Not just me," she whispered. "There are others."

The words slammed through Amelia's chest. Weeks ago, in a room stinking of sweat and iron, a man choked them out while tied to a chair.

There are others.

She thought it might have been a lie, but now she knew it was true.

The girl clutched at Amelia's shirt, her weak fingers digging in like claws. "He…he takes them and sells them." Her voice cracked. "To men…much worse than himself."

Her body buckled with a shiver, her eyes rolling back as another cough tore through her and she sagged against

Amelia's chest.

Lucas's breathing was harsh, fury cutting sharp through every exhale. "This is it," he muttered. His hands curled into fists. "He's really running girls. Just like that bastard said."

Amelia's stomach turned. The air felt thick and choking. Heavy with the perfume that still lingered. Sophia's perfume. It wrapped around her like a noose, dragging her deeper into memory.

Sophia's laughing, then reaching out and bleeding.

Lucas crouched beside her, hands steady but his jaw tense, like holding her together was the only thing stopping him from tearing the world apart.

"We can't keep her here," he said. "If Ethan knows where she went…"

"She'll die if we move her," Amelia cut in. Her words cracked sharper than she meant them to.

Lucas's eyes flicked up, sharp and burning but he didn't say anything.

The storm outside thickened. Rain now hammered against the glass and the wind howled. Amelia pushed to her feet and staggered toward the kitchen sink. Her reflection caught her in the window. Her eyes were sunken and her skin pale. But when she blinked, it wasn't her staring back.

Sophia again. Bruised, broken and lips parting as if she was trying to speak.

Amelia's nails gripped the edge of the counter. "Stop." she whispered. "Please just stop." The whisper came anyway,

He's coming for you.

Her breath stuttered, a rush of panic burning under her

ribs. She turned, searching the kitchen but Lucas's voice cut through before she could lose herself completely.

"Amelia." His tone was sharper than a blade. "Look."

Her gaze followed his to the front door. Something was tucked beneath it, the corner of paper damp from the rain outside.

Lucas snatched the paper from the floor, his eyes narrowing as he read. His fists shook, the paper crumpling under the force of his grip.

He dropped it onto the table. Rain had bled the ink, smearing it a little, but the words were still readable:

You were supposed to make me so much money once you were broken.

But don't worry. I'll have you again.

Amelia's stomach twisted, bile burning the back of her throat. The room tilted. Lucas's breath came rough and dangerous. "That son of a bitch!"

But Amelia couldn't hear him, all she heard was Sophia's laugh echoing through her head.

Three

Chapter 3

The girl was still unconscious, her breath shallow and her skin clammy against the floor. Lucas searched her pockets. His hands found a cheap burner phone. The ringtone cut through the house, neither of them moved at first. Then it rang again. This time Lucas answered it and put it on speaker.

"Sweet Amelia."

Amelia's hands shook against her knees. Tears blurred her vision. "Please," she whispered, voice cracking. "Leave me alone. Haven't you taken enough?"

Ethan's laugh slid down the line, low and poisonous. "Taken enough? You should've made sure I was dead, sweetheart. You should've finished it when you had the chance." His tone darkened. "You were never going to be sold. You were my favourite. Always going to be mine. My bank. Do you understand? Every man with money would've paid for a night. They would've broken you and bought you back to me. And I would've gotten rich of every scream."

Lucas's grip tightened on the phone, his knuckles turned white. Ethan's laugh was jagged, bubbling through the line. "But Lucas, you ruined that, didn't you? You stole her before I had the chance. You cost me a lot of money."

Amelia's chest locked and her hands shook against her knees.

"But don't worry," Ethan whispered down the line. "I'll have her again. No one escapes me. She was worth millions broken. She'll be worth more now."

The line went dead.

Lucas hurled the phone against the wall. The plastic cracked, shards scattering across the floor. His breathing came in ragged bursts, his whole body vibrating with fury.

"Motherfucker!" he snarled.

Amelia's eyes burned, bile rising in her throat. The air was too heavy, Sophia's perfume still lingering in the air, trying to suffocate her.

And then she saw it, headlights through the window. A car across the street, engine idling. Waiting.

"Lucas," she whispered.

He was already moving, knife in his hand and fury in his eyes. He tore open the front door. Rain slashed across his face as the car peeled away. Tires screaming through the wet street.

Lucas stood in the doorway, chest heavy and rain dripping from his fists. He slammed the door so hard the frame rattled.

"I can't fucking sit here," he growled. His voice was a roar under his breath. Dangerous and unraveling. He grabbed his jacket. "I need to bleed this out before it consumes me."

"Lucas please don't leave me right now." Amelia pleaded. But he didn't hear her, he was already gone.

The girl moaned faintly but Amelia couldn't move. She felt so alone without Lucas and she was still trapped under the weight of the perfume. Ethan knew the perfume would mess with her head.

Sophia's voice slid through the dark, haunting Amelia. *"You let me die."*

Her knees gave and she sank against the wall, sobs tearing up her throat. She pressed her hands to her face but it didn't stop the whispers.

You'll die too.

She clawed at the floor until her nails split, the bloody fingers reminding her she was still alive.

* * *

Lucas sat at the bar, shoulders coiled so tight he felt like he might snap in half. Laughter roared, glasses clinked and music vibrated through the floorboards. Every sound scraped at him. The whiskey hit his throat sharp and fast, but it didn't quiet the anger tearing at his insides.

A man bumped into him, shoulder slamming him hard enough to spill the drink over Lucas's knuckles.

Lucas didn't even look up. "Watch it."

The guy turned around, face twisted in irritation. "What the fuck did you say?"

Something inside Lucas snapped tight, sharp enough to cut through the noise. His fists flew before the thought formed, cracking across the man's jaw. The guy staggered, knocking into a table, curses erupting. Chairs scraped. People stood. Lucas didn't care. He lunged again, knuckles slamming into bone.

"Not in here!" the bouncer barked, muscling between them. "Enough. Take it outside or get out."

Lucas's chest heaved. His fists ached. The world blurred into red heat. But instead of dragging the man out, Lucas shoved away from them all. He didn't want this fight. Not this stranger. Not this meaningless shit.

He wanted *Ethan.*

He stormed out into the night, rain slashing his face like needles. The alley behind the bar was empty except for puddles and the echo of the bass thumping through the wall. He braced his hands on his knees, breath tearing out of him. He couldn't go home. Not yet. Not with the fury in him shaped like murder.

A slow drag of shoes on concrete whispered up the alley.

Lucas straightened.

Too late.

A fist cracked into his ribs with the precision of someone who'd been waiting. Pain exploded. Another hit came from the opposite side. He staggered into the wall, shoulder slamming into the brick.

Two men. Dark hoodies.

Ethan's men.

"Boss said to say hello," one hissed, punching Lucas in the jaw. The second jabbed him in the ribs.

"You can't keep her hidden forever, Lucas," the first spat, a cruel grin on his face. "Ethan's been waiting. Can't wait to get

his hands on
Amelia… make her scream again."

"You'll never touch her," Lucas growled, swinging his fist. "Not while I'm breathing." The other slammed a knee into Lucas's stomach. He gasped, tasted blood, and threw an elbow, catching someone's cheekbone with a wet crunch.

A blow landed at the base of his skull. His vision sparked white. He dropped to one knee, fingers digging into wet gravel.

"Tell Amelia we're watching," the second man whispered, breath hot against Lucas's ear.

"Tell her Ethan wants her back."

Another hit. A boot. Pain flared through his ribs. His vision tunnelled. Then footsteps splashed away into the rain.

Lucas stayed on his hands and knees. Fury burned hotter. Sharper. More focused than before.

He wiped the blood from his split lip with the back of his hand.

"Come for me then," he whispered into the rain. "I fucking dare you."

Rain drenched him, mixing with the blood on his knuckles, and he hated himself for leaving her alone. He wanted to be her shield, but he had been too far gone, lost in his own fury.

Four

Chapter 4

Amelia's hands shook so hard she nearly dropped the phone.

"Mason." Her voice cracked. "I need you."

He didn't ask questions. Minutes later, headlights were coming up the driveway.

Amelia yanked the door open before Mason even knocked. The girl's limp body lay crumpled behind her on the floor.

"You need to help me," Amelia gasped. Her voice shook so hard the words barely made it out. "Please, Mason. Help her. Lucas isn't here and I…I don't know what to do."

Mason didn't waste a second; he stepped past her and scooped the girl up like she weighed nothing.

"She'll be safe," he said steady and certain. "I'll get her to the hospital. Nobody will touch her."

Amelia nodded, even though panic was overwhelming her. She clung to the door frame, feeling like her bones couldn't hold her upright.

"Thank you," she whispered.

Mason gave her one last look, something heavy and almost protective behind his eyes and then he turned around and disappeared into the night.

And then the house was silent again. The silence was worse than the storm raging outside.

The perfume still lingered in the air. Sweet and familiar. It crawled over her skin like a living thing, forcing its way into her lungs.

Her chest locked up. Ethan's voice replayed in her mind over and over again. *My bank. Worth millions broken. Loaned out. Used up.*

Her pulse hammered so hard in her chest, it hurt.

Sophia's laughter cut through the silence. It wasn't a real laugh. Her real laugh always lit up the room. This was jagged, broken and haunting.

You let me die.

Amelia staggered, her hands shaking and her legs gave out. She hit the floor hard, her sobs clawed their way out of her chest until she couldn't breathe. She just wanted this to stop.

Her hand found a shard of glass from the burner phone Lucas had smashed. She gripped it tight. The edge bit into her palm, blood welling warm and slick.

She pressed it against her wrist.

Better dead than his.

Her voice was barely a whisper. "I can't. I can't let him take me. I'd rather bleed out right here."

Sophia's shadow lingered in the corner. *You'll die too and it won't matter. You couldn't save me. You can't save yourself.*

Amelia's scream ripped through the room, jagged and raw. She pressed the glass harder, her sobs breaking into sharp, panicked gasps.

Then the door slammed open.

Lucas stood in the doorway, soaked in rain. His fists bruised and bloodied. His chest heaved and he looked almost dangerous.

Then he saw her.

Amelia, curled in the corner and glass trembling against her wrist.

He dropped to the floor beside her. His voice broke. "Amelia."

She flinched back, eyes wide and drowning in tears.

"Why did you leave me?" Her scream split the air. "You promised me, Lucas. You promised I'd never be alone and you left!"

Her sobs shook her entire body. Blood dotted her skin where the shard had bitten in.

"I can't do this," she choked out. "I'd rather die than be his. I'd rather fucking die than let him sell me like meat."

"Don't do this Amelia. Don't leave me like this."

Her body shook harder. Her voice cracked and broken. "You don't get it. I should've saved her. Sophia should still be alive. And you...you walked away and left me like she did."

The words guttered him. His face crumpled and a broken sound tore from his chest.

"I know," he rasped. His eyes burned with something Amelia had never seen in him before.

"I fucked up. I thought I could drown it out, but all I did was abandon you. I wasn't here when you needed me the most. That's on me."

Amelia's grip on the shard faltered. Her wrist trembled and tears streamed hot down her cheeks. Her sobs shredded what was left of her voice. "Then tell me why. Why should I stay? What's the point if I'm already broken? If I'm just going to be his again?"

Lucas crawled closer, inch by inch, like a man begging for mercy. His voice cracked, raw and desperate. "Because you're mine. Because I can't breathe without you. You think I can live if you bleed out in front of me? I'll burn this whole fucking world down before I let him touch you."

The glass slipped from her fingers. It clinked against the floor red smeared across the edge. And then she collapsed into him.

Her sobs tore out of her chest, violent and broken. Lucas wrapped his arms around her, cradling her against him. Pressing her so tight it was like he was trying to fuse her into his bones. His lips pressed against her temple, his breath ragged.

"I'm so sorry," he whispered again and again. "I'm so sorry I wasn't here. I will never leave you again. Not ever."

Amelia buried her face against him, her words muffled against his chest. "Better me dead then be his again."

Lucas's eyes stung, his throat raw.

She swallowed, shaking, trying to push the panic down, but her gaze shifted.

Her eyes fell to his hands, to the bruises spreading under his shirt, the swelling on his jaw.

"Lucas…." Her voice cracked, softer now. "What happened to you?"

He closed his eyes, jaw tight. Every bruise, every cut, every ache a reminder of what he'd faced. His voice came out low, raw. "Nothing that matters...not compared to you."

Amelia shook her head, fury and fear colliding in her chest. "It matters to me!"

He swallowed, voice breaking. "I...I got jumped by some of Ethan's men."

Her hands shook against his chest, and he pulled her in closer.

"This is my fault! I ruined your life! If I hadn't met you, if I hadn't dragged you into my mess, you wouldn't be hurt! You wouldn't...you wouldn't be bleeding for me!"

Her sobs tore through her chest, gasping, ragged. "I should've protected you....I should've killed myself a long time ago then Sophia would still be here and you wouldn't be hurt."

Lucas shook his head, voice low and trembling. "No...no, Amelia. This isn't your fault. I'm here. I'm still here."

Her hands trembled as she pressed against him, trying to hold onto him like he could vanish if she loosened her grip. "But you're hurt...you're hurt because of me!"

He pulled her closer, holding her tight, every ragged breath matching hers. "I'd take every hit again if it meant keeping you alive. I promise, I'm not going anywhere ever again."

Her sobs racked her body, hot and raw, but slowly the tremor in her chest eased, pressed into the solid weight of him.

Five

Chapter 5

She woke in pieces.

Lucas's arm was locked around her like a chain, his grip bruising even in sleep. His chest rose and fell against her back, shallow and uneven. He didn't rest; he anchored.

Her gaze dropped to her wrist. The shard was gone and a strip of gauze wrapped her skin, snug and careful. His work.

For a moment she let herself breathe with him. Pretended it was enough and that the whole world wasn't closing in on her. She was so exhausted still that sleep dragged her under again, quick and merciless.

Sophia stood before her the way she used to. Alive and reckless. Amelia staggered toward her. "I'm sorry," she whispered. "Please forgive me."

Sophia smiled but it cracked. Her throat bloomed with bruises, deep and purple. Blood rimmed her teeth and her voice dropped, wet and wrong.

19

"Why didn't you come?"

Amelia's chest cracked open. She shook her head, reaching out. " I tried…I swear I tried."

Sophia leaned closer, her voice dropping to a whisper. *"He'll make you bleed the way he made me."*

Amelia jolted awake, her heart slamming in her chest.

Lucas was already awake. He hadn't moved but the second her body jolted, his hand was on her shoulder.

"Amelia." His voice low and frayed. "You're safe. It was just a dream."

Her eyes darted, glassy, like she still saw Sophia standing there. He caught her wrist, grounding her. His thumb brushed against the bandage gently.

"I've got you," he murmured, pressing his forehead to hers briefly. "I won't let him touch you again."

But then his jaw clenched until it trembled and the softness cracked. "I should never have sold the penthouse," he said. "Steel. Glass. Security. We were untouchable there. This house has blind corners and too many weak spots."

Her voice cracked. "He got to me there, too. He always gets to me."

His head bowed but she didn't give him mercy.

"I just want him dead," she whispered. "I just want to feel safe again."

Something flickered in his eyes. Not rage. Something colder. The look of a man who'd burn the world if it gave her five seconds of peace.

The silence thickened. Dust floated through the strip of morning light. Her pulse thundered in her ears.

Then, two sharp knocks came at the front door.

Lucas was on his feet instantly, knife in hand. He checked

the peephole. Empty. Only a box sat against the door.

He dragged it in and set it on the table. His eyes never left it.

Cardboard. Tape. Innocent things turned vile.

He cut it open.

Inside lay a dress. Pale and delicate. The soft fabric pretending at innocence. It was her size and folded neat, as if someone had cared enough to press the creases smooth.

Amelia's throat closed and her hands trembled as she reached for it. She expected dirt, blood, something ruined. But the fabric was clean. Waiting.

"What the fuck is this?" Lucas growled. His voice barely human.

Her fingers slipped and the dress spilled from her hands, fabric spreading across the floor.

At the bottom of the box, a phone buzzed to life. Its glow cut through the dim kitchen. Lucas snatched it up and put it on speaker. "Where are you?!"

"Sweet Amelia." Ethan's voice oozed through the speaker. Like poison.

"You'll wear it when I sell you to my buyers," he murmured, soft and intimate. "You'll smile while they break you. You'll beg them to stop, and then you'll beg me for more. You'll come back to me worth more than you ever were alive."

Lucas's eyes burned. "I'll kill you."

Ethan laughed, low and delighted. "You couldn't kill me when I was bleeding out at your estate. You think you'll manage it now? You don't understand Lucas. I don't die. I multiply."

A pause. His breath softer, crueler: "Do you want to know

what Sophia sounded like at the end, Amelia? She screamed your name. Over and over. Each one sweeter than the last. The way her voice cracked when I carved into her. God it was like music to my ears. She died with you on her lips."

Amelia's chest cinched so tight she couldn't breathe. She pressed her hands over her ears, but Ethan's voice seeped through, unstoppable, painting pictures she couldn't erase.

"You'll wear the dress for me," Ethan continued, voice sharpening, almost giddy. "I'll sell you, break you and drag you back. Every bruise will be worth something. And when there's nothing left to sell, you'll still be mine. Because you've always been mine."

Lucas's grip cracked the phone casing in his hand. His voice was a snarl, feral and raw. "I'll ask again, where the fuck are you?!"

That jagged laugh came again. "Closer than you think."

The line clicked dead.

Lucas hurled the phone at the wall. Amelia dropped to her knees, Sophia's eyes flashed in her mind.

"I hate him," she whispered. Her voice broke. "I hate him."

Lucas crouched in front of her, his hands trembling as they cupped her face. His touch was gentle but his eyes were all ash and fire.

"He's going to die," he said. "I promise."

She pressed her forehead against his chest, sobs clawing out of her. His arms closed around her like armor.

Later, when the day bled into night, she dozed on the couch. Lucas hadn't moved. His hand combed through her hair, slow, counting breaths, terrified of missing one.

Her sleep betrayed her.

Sophia stood before her again. Whole at first then broken. Her throat split open as she leaned close, blood bubbling from her lips.

He'll dress you white, so he can watch the red spread.

Amelia jerked awake, a scream splitting from her chest. Lucas caught her, his voice sharp with panic. "I'm here. I'm here."

She clung to him, shaking, eyes cutting into the box.

"All that work," her voice cracked. "The therapy. The fighting. I thought I was done being his victim." Her hands fisted in his shirt. "But I'm not, I'm still pathetic. Still broken. He proves it every time."

Lucas's grip on her tightened. "Don't say that." He angled her chin up, forcing her to see the fury burning in his eyes. "You are not pathetic. You are not broken. He wants you to believe that, he feeds on it. Don't hand it to him."

Her breath shuddered, tears streaking hot down her cheeks. "Then why does it feel like he already owns me.?"

Lucas pressed his forehead to hers, whispering through his teeth. "Because he hasn't seen what happens when you stop running and start fighting. And I swear to you, Amelia, we'll show him."

Six

Chapter 6

Amelia hadn't slept. Every time she closed her eyes, Sophia came for her. Sometimes in the mirror, sometimes in the shadow of the doorway. Always bruised and always bleeding. She saw her in the shine of the kitchen sink, in the glass of the picture frames, and in the reflection of her own pupils.

Sophia didn't vanish when Amelia blinked. She lingered.

Lucas paced the living room, steps restless and muttering under his breath about security. About weak points, about blind corners in the house that could swallow them whole. His voice a low grind, sharp enough to splinter.

Amelia sat on the couch, knees pulled to her chest, feeling the walls press tighter with every step he took. She wanted to tell him to stop, but if he stopped pacing he'd break something instead.

The phone on the table buzzed. Mason's name lit the screen.

Lucas answered. Mason didn't waste any time.

"The girl woke up. She's weak, but she said something."

Amelia leaned forward, clinging to the sound of his voice. "What?"

"She said Ethan always knew where you were. Always. Like he had eyes inside the house."

Mason's pause was heavy. "You know what that means."

Lucas froze mid-step. His jaw locked, a muscle ticking near his temple. "A mole."

The word cut the air.

His eyes burned as he looked at Amelia. "I knew it. The cameras in the estate. The way Ethan always knew where to hit us. I told myself maybe I was wrong, but this…" he dragged a hand through his hair, "this just confirms it."

Amelia's skin crawled. She wrapped her arms tighter around her knees. Her gaze drifted to the window, half expecting Sophia's face to be staring back from the glass.

After they hung up, Lucas shoved his hands through his hair, breathing sharp. "One of mine has been feeding him information and watching us."

"Lucas…." Amelia tried, but her voice broke.

He didn't hear her, already pacing again, faster as he muttered under his breath.

She curled tighter, nails digging against the gauze wrapped around her wrist. The itch beneath it burned, a reminder of the shard she'd pressed against her skin.

Without thinking, her fingers slipped under the edge of the bandage, scratching until her skin stung. The sting helped. It made her feel anchored.

Mason's words still hung in the air. *He always knew where you were.*

Amelia's throat closed. She pulled her sleeve down quick when she heard Mason's truck outside.

The front door creaked open. Mason stepped in, eyes moving from Lucas's pacing form to Amelia curled on the couch. He didn't miss the way her hands shook as she smoothed her sleeve.

"You holding up?" he asked quietly.

She forced a nod. "Fine."

Mason lingered, thumb dragging over the scar on his knuckle like he was swallowing the urge to kneel beside her. He'd known Lucas long enough to read the storm in his shoulders, to know when to step in and when to let him burn it out. So he moved instead—checked the locks, adjusted the curtains, the kind of quiet care that said he saw them both unraveling and was trying to keep the world from getting in while they did.

He came back, voice low. "You two need sleep. I'll take first watch."

Lucas didn't answer.

Mason sighed under his breath. "Didn't think so." His eyes softened when they met Amelia's again, a silent promise tucked inside the look: *I've got you both.*

Lucas snapped, dragging their attention back. "We find the mole. We end him. Then we go for Ethan." His voice was a vow, sharp enough to bleed on.

Amelia just pressed her sleeve tighter against her wrist. Sophia's reflection flickered in the dark glass of the TV, her dead eyes staring back like she already knew how this would end.

Seven

Chapter 7

Lucas had them lined up in the living room. His men. His empire. They stood shoulder to shoulder, silent, backs rigid. The storm outside had passed, but inside the house the air was thick, charged, like it could snap with the one wrong word. Lucas prowled in front of them, the knife loose in his grip. He spun it between his fingers, blade catching the light with each turn. His voice came quiet, even. That was worse than yelling. "One of you fed him. One of you let Ethan inside my walls. The cameras at the estate. The doors unlocked. You think I didn't see it?"

No answer. The silence pressed tight, suffocating.

Lucas stopped in front of one man, close enough that the

point of the knife tapped against his chest. "You know what happens to traitors? You don't get a grave. You get erased."

The man's Adam's apple bobbed.

Amelia sat curled on the couch, knees hugged tight, heart pounding. She wanted to scream at him to stop, but her throat locked. He looked like a storm barely contained in skin, rage simmering just beneath the surface.

One of the men swallowed, too loud.

Lucas moved instantly, knife at his throat. The man froze, blood beading where the edge kissed his skin.

"Lucas!" Amelia lurched forward, voice cracking. "Stop!"

His head snapped toward her, eyes burning. "Don't!" His tone was quiet but lethal. "Don't tell me how to protect you." He turned back to his men. "He knew where she was. What she wore. How she smelled. One of you gave him that. One of you handed her to him."

Amelia's chest clenched, bile rising in her throat. Mason's voice cut through, steady but edged. "You tear your crew apart, you'll have nothing left to fight with. That's what Ethan wants. He's already in your head. Don't hand him the rest."

For a moment, Lucas didn't move. His jaw flexed, the knife trembling in his grip. Then, with a sudden snap, he drove the blade into the table. Wood splintered, glass rattled.

"Get out!" he growled.

The men scattered, boots hammering the stairs, relief written across every face.

The silence that followed was heavier than their presence. Lucas dragged his hands down his face, pacing again, muttering under his breath. About locks, about corners, and about betrayal. Each word grated raw, like he was chewing on glass.

His fists opened and closed, veins standing out sharp in his forearms. Amelia pulled her sleeve down tighter, scratching beneath the gauze until the sting burned. The pain steadied her. Lucas's words echoed. *He always knew where you were.*

***

That night, the house was too still. Amelia drifted into sleep and Sophia was waiting.

She stood at the foot of the bed, bright at first. Reckless grin. Spark in her eyes. Then the bruises bloomed around her throat, deep purple like invisible fingers digging into her skin. Blood spilled from her mouth, soaking down her chest. Her lips parted, opening wider, wider. But no sound came out.

Amelia reached for her, desperation choking her. "Please, please say something."

But Sophia only bled, silent.

Amelia jolted awake, lungs clawing for air. Sweat slicked her skin. Her heart thundered like it wanted to crack her ribs.

Her hand fumbled for the drawer. The blade was there, cool and certain. She gripped it tight, pressed the edge against her wrist. The relief was instant, dizzying, as the blood welled red in the dark.

The lamp snapped on.

"What the fuck do you think you're doing?"

Lucas's voice split the silence. He was already on her, ripping the blade from her hand and hurling it across the room. His grip clamped her wrist, dragging it up so the fresh cut glistened under the light.

His thumb pressed into it, hard until she cried out. Blood

smeared between his fingers. "You think this makes you free?"

His voice was jagged and feral.

"You think bleeding will keep him out of your head? You think it will make her stop haunting you?"

Tears streaked down Amelia's cheeks, her body trembling.

"I can't....She is everywhere. Sophia's everywhere."

His thumb ground into the cut until she whimpered, blood smearing between his fingers. "You don't bleed for ghosts. You don't bleed for him." His forehead pressed to hers, his breath uneven, almost breaking. "If you bleed, it's for me. Only me."

Her breath hitched, sobs catching.

"Say it," he demanded, low, guttural, vibrating through her bones. "Say who you belong to."

Her lips trembled. "You."

A dark sound broke out of him, more pain than rage. His mouth crashed against hers, brutal and desperate. Biting until she tasted copper. One hand pinned her wrists above her head, the other slid down, possessive, claiming, making sure she remembered she was still alive, still his. His forehead pressed to hers hard enough to hurt, his breath shaking. "Don't make me watch you disappear."

She gasped when his fingers found her clit, circling hard and merciless until a moan broke from her throat. He swallowed the sound, devouring her.

Without warning, he released his cock from his pants and slammed into her, the stretch brutal and holy, tearing another cry from her throat.

"Mine," he growled, thrusting deep, fast, relentless, each snap of his hips punishing. "Say it again."

Her scream fractured, tears streaking down her cheeks. "Yours!"

His grip slid from her wrists to her throat, squeezing just enough to choke her breath, forcing her gaze to his. His eyes were wild, burning through her, as if he could brand the word into her very bones.

"You belong to me. Not Ethan. Not your ghosts. Me."

Her body shattered beneath him, climax ripping through her in waves, sobs spilling into the dark as she screamed his name.

He followed with a guttural snarl, spilling inside her as he crushed her to the mattress, still holding her throat, still pinning her like he could weld her into his skin.

When silence returned, Amelia's gaze drifted toward the corner of the room.

Sophia was there. Her mouth open, blood dripping silently down her chin.

Amelia blinked, and she was gone.

But the cut burned beneath Lucas's thumb. And his voice stayed in her ear, low and relentless: *Mine.*

Chapter 8

Morning broke thin and grey.

Amelia lay on her back, wrist freshly bandaged, the sheets clinging to her skin. Lucas was already awake. Shirtless. Barefoot. Knife resting on the table beside him. He sat hunched over the laptop, eyes fixed on the camera feeds.

He hadn't slept. His jaw worked like stone, shoulders rigid.

"Windows stay latched," he muttered, not to her. "Back door gets a new deadbolt. We rotate routes, no patterns, no tells. Cameras…"

His voice cut off.

"What is it?" she asked, pushing up on her elbows.

He leaned closer. On the garage feed the picture hiccuped. Clear then snow, then black. It came back two minutes later like nothing had happened. Lucas scrolled back, frame by frame, eyes gone flat and bright.

"Somebody cut it," he said, voice low enough to shake the

room. "They knew which line, which camera. Not random. Inside."

By nine, two of his men were standing in the kitchen, stiff-backed and silent. Lucas paced in front of them with the knife loose in his grip, the point ticking the counter like a metronome.

He turned the laptop so they could see the frozen rectangle of static.

"Here," he said, too calm. "Two minutes. Gone. Where were you when this happened?"

They traded a look. One started to speak, stumbled. "We… we were at the north gate. Sir, I swear."

Lucas had him by the throat before the second word finished, slammed him against the pantry door, knife under his chin.

"You don't swear," he said, voice almost gentle. "You prove, where were you when my camera died?"

The man's breath hitched. "I don't..I was.."

"Lucas." Amelia stepped forward, palms raised though they shook. "Stop."

His eyes snapped to her, then back to the man. The knife pressed harder, a bead of blood welling bright against skin. "Every mistake they make puts a blade closer to your throat," he said without looking away from her. "And I don't forgive that. Ever."

Amelia moved closer, pressing her hand against his chest. Her voice cracked. "Please."

For a moment the air fractured with the possibility he wouldn't listen. His jaw clenched, the knife trembled against flesh.

Then, slowly, he pulled it back, dragging a shallow line down the man's collar before stepping away.

The man sagged against the door, choking on air.

Lucas turned, catching Amelia's wrist, pulling her toward him. His voice was a growl, sharp enough to flay. "He breathes because you told me to stop. Not because I would've."

He ripped the knife from the wall. "Get out."

Lucas dragged a hand through his hair until it stood on end. "He's already inside," he said to the air. "Blind corners. Weak locks. Every one of them a mouth for him to climb through."

Amelia folded her arms around herself. The bandage tugged as she moved, the itch under it pulsed. She dug her nails above the gauze until the sting made a small, bright place to live in.

The afternoon dragged like wet cement, Lucas stayed hunched over the table, mapping names, lines, routes. His pen carved hard into paper until the wood beneath scored. Amelia lingered on the edges, watching him chew through every possibility like a man gnawing bone.

Mason returned with food, containers sweating on the counter. "Eat," he said flat, sliding one toward Amelia.

She peeled the lid off, steam curling into the air. The smell hit wrong, sour in her throat. She tried to lift a forkful, but her stomach rolled. She pushed it away.

"I can't," she whispered.

The scrape of Lucas's chair was louder than her voice. He came up behind her, leaned down until his mouth brushed her ear. His breath was hot, his words low and final.

"No, Amelia. You need to eat."

The command, slithered through her like chains.

Her hands shook as she lifted another bite. She forced it down, gagged and bolted to the sink. The sound of her retching filled the silence.

Mason started forward, but Lucas caught her first, palm spread between her shoulder blades, steadying.

His jaw was locked tight, eyes burning with something that wasn't quiet anger and wasn't quiet fear.

She rinsed her mouth, wiped her lips with the back of her trembling hand. "It's just stress," she muttered, voice hoarse. "That's all."

Lucas didn't answer. He pressed a glass of water into her hand, fingers lingering too long, eyes narrowing like he could see through her skin.

The shadows stretched as the day dimmed, filling the corners, crawling long across the walls. Amelia caught herself staring at them too long, convinced one of them would move.

In the glass of the blackened TV, Sophia flicked. Not solid, just suggestion, the tilt of her head, the drip of red.

Amelia blinked hard until it was only her pale reflection.

By the time Lucas finally pushed back from the table, the sky outside had collapsed into night. His body was tight, every line of him wound too sharp.

"Bed," he said, not a suggestion.

Amelia hadn't meant to speak, but the words slipped free anyway jagged with tears. "I can't do this. I'll fall apart."

Lucas's arm locked around her waist, dragging her into his lap like he was afraid she might vanish if he let go. His mouth brushed her ear, voice low and raw. "Then fall apart here. With me. You don't run, not in your head, not in your skin. You stay."

Her pulse hammered, chest shuddering against his. "What if I'm not strong enough?"

His grip tightened, one hand covering the bandage at her wrist, sealing, it like a vow. His forehead pressed to hers, eyes burning into her. "You don't need to be. You live because I love you. That's the one thing he can't take. He can't touch what's mine to protect."

Her lips trembled, breath stuttering against his.

"Say it," he ordered, voice vibrating through her bones. Her throat closed, but the word tore out anyway. "Yours."

His mouth crashed against hers, brutal and unrelenting, his teeth scraping until she gasped. He swallowed the sound whole, his tongue devouring her, his hand shoving between her thighs to drag her open.

Her moan broke raw into his mouth.

"That's it," he muttered, against her lips. "No hiding, not from me."

His fingers circled her clit, slow and cruel, building her until she trembled, until she clawed at his shoulders. Every whimper, every shift of her hips, he denied her, holding her in place until she was desperate.

When she tried to grind down harder, he pulled his hand away and gripped her throat, thumb pressing under her jaw until her head tipped back. "Not until I say."

"Lucas…"

He freed himself, thick and hard against her, dragging the head of his cock, smearing her wetness, teasing her entrance without giving her the relief she needed.

Her body arched, begging without words.

He grinned, merciless, before pushing inside, slow, inch by inch, forcing her to take every stretch, every drag.

She moaned, head falling back, throat exposed in his grip.

He bottomed out and held her there, buried deep, refusing

to move. His gaze burned into hers, wild and reverent all at once. "Eyes on me. I want you to remember who keeps you breathing."

When he finally began to move , it was punishing and controlled. Slow drags that pushed her higher, then stops that left her shaking. He wrung sound from her, sobs twisting into moans, each thrust claiming more of her.

"Say it again," his pace quickened, brutal now.

Her nails raked down his back, desperate. "Yours Lucas always!"

The words broke on a scream as she shattered, pleasure tearing through her like glass. Her body convulsed around him, her sobs ripped raw.

He groaned into her mouth, hips snapping harder, spilling inside her as he held her down on his cock, forcing her to take every drop.

Even when it was over, he didn't let her go. He kept her locked in his lap, cock still buried in her, his hand gripping her jaw so she had no choice but to meet his eyes.

"You don't get to break," he whispered, harsh and intimate. "You stay here. With me. Always."

When sleep finally dragged her under, it was thin and mean. The kind that barely soothed, only reminded her how exhausted she really was. Shadows pooled behind her eyelids.

Somewhere in the distance, thunder cracked. Her body floated, restless, always half-ready to wake.

Hours slipped by like whispers.

She woke to the scrape of a chair and found the bed empty, Lucas bent over the laptop again with the lamp low. The knife lay beside the keyboard.

"What now?" Her voice was bone-dry.

He froze the garage feed and leaned close. "There." He tapped the screen with a knuckle. "Headlights. Two a.m. Parked across the street. No engine on the audio, so it's idling far back, not ours."

She pushed herself upright, adrenaline souring her mouth. "Maybe it's a neighbour."

He shook his head. "The same car shows up at one forty-one the night before. Leaves at two am. Same angle. Same wait."

"How long?" She didn't know if she meant the car or the sentence she was living inside.

"Long enough to watch when the lights go off in our bedroom." His voice had no air in it. "Long enough to learn our breath."

On the screen, the frozen frame made the glow look like eyes. Watching the house breathe.

He shut the laptop like it offended him. The room went darker.

"He's already here," Lucas said.

And it didn't sound like fear. It sounded like a blade being unsheathed.

Nine

Chapter 9

Lucas hadn't stopped moving since the headlights.

The world outside their house had turned into a hunting ground, and he refused to sit still and wait for Ethan to take the next shot. Not this time. Mason drove with his jaw locked, eyes pinned to the road. Two more of their men followed in another car.

Lucas sat in the passenger seat with a knife balanced in his palm, turning it and testing the edge against his skin until a bead of blood rose. The sting pinned his mind into a single, lethal line.

The docks greeted them with cold that crawled beneath clothes. Rot clung to the water, rust and oil thick enough to taste. Lucas stalked between stacked containers, silent, focused. The first man they caught tried to run. Lucas slammed him into a crate hard enough that the metal shuddered, ribs snapping like cheap wood. His hand wrapped around the man's throat.

"Where's bird?" Lucas growled.

The man choked out excuses. Lucas's fist erased them. Blood sprayed the crate, a wet slap in the night. Mason grabbed Lucas's shoulder, but Lucas tore free and kept hitting until the man's head lolled and teeth skittered across the concrete.

"You think I'm playing?" Lucas snarled. "Tell me where he is, or I'll cut your tongue out and feed it to the gulls."

The man sobbed, coughing red. "Locker 14… white van… scar through his brow. They call him bird."

Lucas slammed him once more, because stopping on command wasn't something he did.

Then he let the body crumble.

"If you're lying, I'll come back for you."

They searched the lockers. Fourteen waited for them like a dare, burner phone taped to the wall a folded note inside. Mason peeled it off. The scrawl was uneven. Two A.M. Bay six. Confirm pickup.

Lucas's mouth curved, sharp. "Good. He's not a ghost. He keeps schedule." The white van rolled in at one-forty. Lucas spotted it from across the yard, the dented panel, the profile, the scar splitting the brow. Bird. His pulse roared. He stepped forward. Mason caught his arm. "Not yet. We don't have the crew. We don't know who else is watching."

Lucas's jaw ticked, rage caged beneath his teeth. His body screamed for violence. His mind screamed for Ethan's head on the concrete. He forced himself back. Barely.

When the van slipped away, Lucas's vow filled the cold. "Next time, he doesn't leave breathing."

* * *

Amelia sat curled on the couch, the house too still around her. Every tick of the clock dragged, slow and heavy. She shoved her hands into her sleeves, stomach twisting on itself. Twice she ran to the bathroom, gagging over nothing. The taste of bile clung to her tongue. She told herself it was fear. Just fear.

Sophia hovered again in the dark glass of the TV, closer than before. Bruised. Bloodied. Her mouth opening in a silent scream.

"I know," she whispered. "I know he's coming."

Headlights washed over the wall. A car in the driveway. Her pulse seized. She held her breath as the door opened.

Lucas stepped inside, blood dried across his knuckles, fog clinging to his jacket. His eyes burned with something that looked like victory stretched thin over madness.

Relief and fear twisted so tight inside her she couldn't separate them. Her stomach lurched. She bolted to the bathroom, retching until her ribs trembled.

Lucas was there instantly, dropping to his knees beside her. His bloody hand pressed between her shoulder blades, steady, rough and grounding.

"Are you okay?" His voice was harsh, but it wasn't anger. It was fear wearing armor.

She wiped her mouth with her sleeve, shaking. "Don't you miss it?" Her voice cracked.

"Who we were when we first met? When it wasn't like this?"

Lucas stilled. For a heartbeat he didn't breathe.

Then his gaze speared through her.

"That was a long time ago," he said. His thumb brushed her

temple, gently.

"Back when my rage was in check. Back when we didn't live this nightmare."

Amelia leaned into him, trembling, breath thin, the bathroom stinking of bile and memory.

Lucas pulled her closer and for a moment, for one fragile moment, they were the only two people left in the world.

Ten

Chapter 10

The house felt different in the morning. Not safer. Just quieter. A silence that pressed down on Amelia's chest until every breath scraped.

She moved through the kitchen like a ghost. The smell of coffee turned her stomach. She barely made it to the sink before bile scorched her throat. She clutched porcelain, trembling, whispering to herself that it was nerves. Stress. Nothing else.

Behind her, the floor creaked.

Lucas's shadow filled the doorway. His jacket hung open, shirt crumpled, blood still dried across the back of his knuckles. His eyes cut to her like blades. "You're sick."

"I'm fine." The lie snapped too fast, too sharp.

He crossed the room in two strides, hand catching her jaw, tilting her face toward him. His eyes burned. "Don't lie to me. Not about this. Not about anything."

Her throat locked. She wanted to protest, but no words came.

He pressed his forehead to hers, breath unsteady like he was fighting the urge to wrap her in every part of himself. His hand cupped her jaw, firm but careful, guiding her gaze back to him.

"Look at me," he murmured. "I need you here."

Her eyes met his, fragile and flickering.

"You'll eat," he said, voice low. "You'll drink water. You'll stay on your feet. Not because I'm ordering you around." His thumb stroked the edge of her cheekbone. "Because I can't lose you."

She nodded, small and trembling. "That's not enough." His tone softened into something that felt like a warning and a promise all at once. "Say it so I know you're not disappearing on me."

"I'll do it," she whispered.

Lucas exhaled like that single sentence unclenched something inside him. His thumb brushed her lip, lingering with a reverence that bordered on devotion.

"Good girl." His forehead leaned harder onto hers. "You're mine to protect."

He guided her to the table with a steadiness she didn't have, lowering her into the chair like she might slip through the cracks, if he wasn't careful. He poured the water himself, setting the glass in front of her before placing her hand around it. Her fingers trembled, barely holding on.

His hand slid over hers, warm and anchoring. He lifted both their hands together until the rim touched her mouth. His voice dropped to something meant only for her.

"Breathe. Then drink. I've got you."

She swallowed, gagged once, but it stayed down. His hand stayed wrapped around hers. "You don't get to vanish on me," he murmured. "Not to him. Not to your ghosts. Not ever to yourself."

Her eyes burned. She pressed her forehead against his chest, weak and trembling. He stroked her hair, slow. "Whatever this sickness is, we will deal with it. But you'll obey me. You'll eat, you'll sleep because I won't bury you. Do you hear me? I won't."

Her stomach twisted again. She nodded, silent.

The phone buzzed on the counter. Lucas's hand shot out, snatching it.

Mason's voice filled the line. "We've got him. Bird. Bay six. Tonight."

Lucas's lips curved in a dark, hungry smile. His grip on Amelia tightened. "Good. I want his blood on my hands."

Amelia closed her eyes, Sophia's reflection burned behind them.

When she opened them again, Lucas was already pulling away.

"Don't," she whispered, fingers catching his wrist. "Please. Don't go. Not yet."

He froze.

The man who'd just promised violence replaced, only for a heartbeat by the one who held her together when she splintered. He cupped the back of her head, pressing his forehead to hers.

"I know, sweetheart." His voice cracked with a softness he

rarely let anyone hear. "I know, you don't want to be alone right now."

"Stay," she begged, voice small and shaking. "Just stay with me."

His jaw flexed. A war raged behind his eyes; comfort her, destroy the man who'd ruined her life. He brushed a thumb under her eye, catching a tear before it fell.

"If I stay," he murmured, "he walks free a little longer."

Her breath hitched.

"And I can't let that happen," he finished, voice turning to steel again. "Not after what he did. Not after what he stole."

Amelia's fingers tightened around him, but Lucas gently pried them loose, kissing her knuckles like a goodbye he didn't want to give.

A jagged fear twisted through her chest, the old gnawing terror that this time, he might not come back. Or worse, that the violence would steal what was left of him and send back a stranger wearing his face.

"I'm coming back to you," he promised. "And when I do, this part of your story ends."

A single tear slid down her cheek, as she watched him walk out the door.

* * *

The docks stank of rust and tide.

Bird was already tied to a chair when Lucas stepped from the shadows. The scar through his brow was as ugly as the rumors. Blood streaked his face. Mason's men had softened him up. But Lucas wanted more than bruises.

He crouched low, knife flashing in the dim light. "You've been watching my house. Feeding him. Where's Ethan?"

Bird spat blood onto the concrete. "Closer than you think."

Lucas's fist cut the words off. He slammed the man's head back against the chair until teeth rattled. The knife tip traced a line down his cheek, shallow, deliberate. "Wrong answer."

What followed wasn't quick. Lucas broke him piece by piece. Fingers bent back until they snapped, ribs cracked under the heel of his boot. Questions carved into flesh, each refusal answered with pain. Mason stood in the corner, jaw tight, letting it happen.

At last, Bird broke. Choking, sobbing, he spat up names, routes, drop points. Two handlers who answered directly to Ethan. Ledgers passed hand to hand. Buyers waiting overseas.

Lucas didn't stop when he had what he needed. He leaned in close, voice almost tender. "Do you know why you're dying tonight?"

Bird's eyes rolled, broken and wet.

"Because you touched what's mine."

The blade opened his throat in one smooth motion. Blood poured over concrete, pooling black in the shadows. Lucas stood over him, breathing hard, steady, empty.

"Clean it," he told the men, tossing the knife aside. Mason didn't argue.

The house was silent when he returned.

Lucas climbed the stairs slow, shoulders heavy. In their bedroom, he found Amelia asleep for the first time in weeks. Deep, dreamless, her face slack with peace. Beside the bed, a sick bucket sat on the floor, proof of what she'd fought through to get there.

He stripped quietly, sliding into bed beside her. She stirred faintly when he pulled the blanket over them both, but didn't wake.

Lucas pressed his chest to her back, arm heavy around her waist, caging her close. His nose touched her hairline, and he let himself breathe her in. For a heartbeat, the blood and screams at the docks threatened to claw their way between them. He held her tighter, desperate to drown out the monster with the warmth of her skin.

"You're safe," he whispered into her sleep. "As long as I breathe, you're safe."

His grip tightened. His eyes stayed open and for a few hours, he let her steady breathing anchor the monster he'd been at the docks.

Eleven

Chapter 11

Lucas replayed the docks.

He scrubbed the footage back to the minute Bird's throat opened and watched the world around it instead, the cranes like crooked fingers, the fog breathing, the way the corner camera hiccuped for three seconds right before the van slid into frame. It shouldn't have hiccuped. Not there. Not then.

"Someone touched my eyes," he said voice flat.

Mason leaned on the doorway, arms folded, face unreadable. "You sure it's not the weather?"

Lucas froze the frame. He magnified the timestamp. Then the access log he'd pulled from the garage panel. A maintenance ping. Badge authorisation at 01:32. He didn't schedule maintenance. The badge belonged to one of his own.

"Get me Riley. And Jase." Lucas said, "Now!"

They stood in the mudroom ten minutes later, boots damp, faces open in the way people think makes them look innocent.

Lucas didn't sit. He moved. Knife in hand, rolling it across his knuckles until it hummed. He turned the laptop to them, tapped the screen. "This," he said, "three seconds of snow. And this, the access log, it's your badge Riley. You want to tell me why my cameras blinked when Bird arrived?"

Riley swallowed. "I didn't… I didn't sir. I've got no reason to."

Lucas hit him hard enough to tear the lie out by the root. Riley's head snapped, blood misting his lips.

"Try again."

"I was on the north lot," Riley said, voice too fast. "Jase can…"

Jase flinched, eyes cutting anywhere but Lucas's. "We were… we were switching patrol. I don't know about any…"

Lucas slammed Riley into the wall and drove the knife into the plaster beside his ear.

"You don't 'don't know' in my house!"

Mason's jaw tightened. He didn't step in. Not yet.

Lucas's voice softened, terrifying because of it. "You text when our bedroom goes dark too? Count breaths for him? He likes that. Learning rhythm. Predicting when I close my eyes." He dragged the blade down, slow, shaving a curl of paint. "What did he promise you, Riley? Money? Safety? A cut when he sold her?"

Riley's throat worked, his gaze flicked to Amelia's band of light under the hallway door and something flickered across his face. Guilt.

"Talk." Lucas yelled.

Jase broke first. "Ethan paid him," he blurted out. "Cash. Envelopes in the utility box behind the east gate. I swear to

God, Lucas, he said it was just whereabouts. Lights on, lights off. A car or two. That's it. He said it was nothing."

Riley went white. "Shut up."

Lucas didn't look at Jase again. He pressed the knife to Riley's chest until it dimpled meat and opened a small, mean line. Blood ran thin.

"How much?" Lucas asked. "For her."

Riley's jaw clenched. "He.. he said she was worth more broken. He said ten percent if the sale went through. I never… I didn't think."

"You didn't think because you don't have a brain," Lucas said. "You have a hole where one should live."
The hall floor creaked. Amelia stood there, sleeve pulled over her bandaged wrist, skin grey under the kitchen light. Sleep still clung to her, delicate and stubborn. Her eyes found the blood on Riley's face, then Lucas's hand, then the knife.

"Lucas," she said softly, the plea raw at the edges, "don't."

He turned his head enough to see her. Something in him flinched. Then he turned back to Riley like he couldn't trust himself to look twice.

"You sold my house," Lucas said low. "You sold her breath. You sold my sleep. You breathed with us and handed him the count."

"I'm sorry," Riley whispered, and it was real, which made Lucas want to tear his throat out more.

"No," Lucas said. "You're sorry *you were caught.*"

He moved the knife from Riley's cheek to his mouth, the flat of the blade against his lips.

"Open," Lucas said.

Riley shook. He opened. The steel slid inside and tasted his teeth.

"Lucas," Amelia said again, her voice shaking. "Please."

His eyes didn't leave Riley's. "He was promised a cut," Lucas said, his voice breaking as he spat the words. He finally turned, looked at Amelia, his face twisted with rage and grief. "Do you hear me? He was going to get paid when you were sold. When you were screaming. When you were broken."

Amelia staggered back, the words cutting deeper than the knife ever could.

Then he shoved the knife upward.

Steel punched through the soft palate, driving deep until the point bust out just beneath Riley's brow. Blood sprayed hot across Lucas's hand as Riley's eyes went wide, body convulsing. A wet gargle tore from his throat, echoing through the room.

Amelia screamed, hands flying to her mouth, tears flooding down her face.

Lucas held him steady, forcing him to look at him even as the life drained out of him. "This is what he thought you were worth," Lucas hissed. "A transaction."

He dropped the knife free. Riley collapsed in a twitching heap, blood flooding the floor, his mouth frozen in a half-formed plea.

Lucas turned toward Amelia, chest heaving, hands and face streaked red. His voice cracked as he spoke, rough but unwavering.

"You'll never be a sale. Never a cut. Not while I breathe."

He didn't look away from her until he had to. Then he snapped toward Mason and Jase, voice sharp enough to peel skin.

"Clean him up. Get him out of my sight. Burn what's left."

Jase nodded too fast, swallowing bile. Mason just grunted,

calm in the storm.

When Lucas's gaze found Amelia again, she was shaking from the adrenaline crash, knuckles white on the sink, bile still burning on her tongue. But her eyes held him, steady and furious and also terrified for him.

"You can't keep doing this," she whispered, voice raw. "You'll burn yourself alive before anyone else gets the chance."

Lucas crossed the room in two steps, blood still dripping from his hands. She didn't flinch. Didn't retreat. She lifted her chin even as her body trembled.

His palms cupped her face. He pressed his forehead to hers, breath ragged against her cheek.

"I won't let the world take you. Ever."

Amelia's fingers curled around his wrists, holding him there, grounding him.

"I know," she breathed. "But let me keep you too."

Twelve

Chapter 12

Lucas hadn't moved from the chair by the bed, knife balanced across his thigh, watching Amelia sleep. Every time her breathing stuttered, he thought about Riley's face, the way the blade had burst out through the bone. He thought about how she'd looked at him after.

When the pale light came through the curtains, he finally rose. The kitchen was too quiet.

His hands trembled as he made breakfast for Amelia, eggs sizzling, toast browning. Simple rituals grounding him while everything felt like it was falling apart.

He carried the tray upstairs, the smell of coffee rising warm in the air.

Amelia stirred when he set the tray down. Her lashes fluttered, heavy with sleep, and she blinked at him like she wasn't sure if he was real.

"I'm sorry you had to see that side of me, yesterday." Lucas said crouching low, thumb brushing the hair from her face. His voice broke, soft. "But I'll do anything to protect you, Amelia. You're the love of my life. I won't lose you."

Her throat moved like she might answer, but the words never came. She clapped a hand to her mouth and lurched for the bucket by the bed.

Her body heaved, violent, spilling bile until her shoulders shook.

"Fuck." Lucas grabbed the bucket, his other hand gathering her hair back. He pressed a glass of water into her trembling fingers. "You need a doctor. Something's wrong."

She shook her head, wiping her mouth on her sleeve. "It's just stress. I'm fine."

He didn't believe her. His jaw locked, rage simmering under the surface, but he didn't argue.

* * *

The morning was too still.

Then came the roar.

Tires on gravel. Engine screaming down the street.

Lucas's head snapped up. "Down!" he barked, shoving Amelia flat against the mattress and covering her body with his.

Gunfire shattered the silence. Bullets ripped through the windows, glass exploding across the floor. The walls shuddered as plaster dust filled the air. A lamp toppled, shattering. The smell of gunpowder bled into the room, sharp and choking. Lucas covered her, every muscle locked, his breath hot in her hair.

The car's engine faded, tires squealing as it vanished into the distance.

Silence. Only the ringing in their ears.

Lucas stood slowly, glass crunching under his boots. His eyes burned, wild and murderous, as he scanned the ruined windows. "He was here." His voice raw, shaking. "Close enough to see her face."

Amelia curled tighter into the sheets, tears streaking her cheeks. "He'll never stop." She whispered.

Lucas turned back to her, jaw trembling. "Then neither will I."

Lucas's breathing was a growl as he yanked his phone out of his pocket. "Mason. I want men here now. Windows replaced, every inch of this house locked down. I want eyes on every corner until it's a fortress."

On the other end Mason's voice was clipped, steady. "I'll handle it."

Lucas ended the call without another word. His gaze snapped back to Amelia, still curled on the bed, trembling. He crossed the room, crouched beside her, brushing shards of glass from the sheets before lifting her chin.

"You hurt?" His voice cracked, desperation barely hidden under the grit.

Her head shook fast. No. Just..." She bolted upright, barely catching the bucket in time as her stomach heaved again.

Violent gut-deep retches, wracked her body until she was gasping, tears spilling down her face.

Lucas held her hair back, jaw locked, helpless rage bleeding into his grip. "This isn't just stress. Something's wrong, Amelia."

"I said I'm fine," she snapped between breaths, though her voice was weak. "It's just stress. That's all."

"You need a doctor."

"No." Her voice cracked out, her whole body still shaking.

Lucas bit back the fury, swallowing it into silence. His hands never left her back, steady against each tremor.

The phone on the bedside table buzzed.

Lucas snatched it up, eyes narrowing at the unknown number. He answered on speaker "Where are you?!"

Ethan's laugh slithered through, smooth and cruel. "Relax, Lucas. If I wanted her hurt she'd already be bleeding in your arms. That was just a little reminder. To show you I'm close. Close enough to count the freckles on her face when she ducked under you."

Amelia froze, bile rising in her throat again.

"You'll never touch her," Lucas snarled. His grip on the phone tightened.

"Oh but I will," Ethan murmured, almost tender. "Not with a bullet. Guns are messy. Amelia deserves better than that. I'll take my time. Break her. Sell her scream by scream until she beds me to make her mine again."

Amelia's sobs tore from her chest, raw and jagged.

Lucas's voice shook, murderous. "I'll cut you into pieces before that happens."

Ethan chuckled. "We'll see. It won't be long."

The line went dead.

Thirteen

Chapter 13

Ethan's voice followed her into sleep.

White dress. Red Stains. Scream for me, Amelia. Scream like she did.

She clawed awake, chest heaving, the echo of his laughter still gnawing her bones. Sweat slicked her skin. Sophia's reflection hovered in the glass of the dresser, throat split, lips moving without sound.

Amelia's hand fumbled for the shard hidden in the drawer. Cold. Familiar. She dragged it across her wrist, pain slicing sharp, blood rising fast and hot. For a heartbeat, it felt like control.

Lucas burst through the doorway, his heart already pounding, but when he saw the blood, saw Amelia hunched over with the glass pressed to her skin, the world seemed to stop. For a split second, all the breath was ripped from his chest.

"Amelia?" His voice cracked, softer than a whisper. He

crossed the room in an instant, the sight of blood making his hands shake as he dropped to his knees beside her.

"What were you thinking?" He gently but firmly pried the shard from her hand. Blood smeared across his fingers.

"Amelia, please," he breathed, voice trembling as he grabbed a towel and pressed it to her wrist. "Why would you do this? You're scaring me."

He held her hand tight, his whole body shaking as he tried to stop the bleeding, his eyes wild with panic and desperate care.

"You don't have to do this alone. I'm right here. Let me help, baby."

Her sobs broke open, violent, shaking. " I can't… I can't breathe. He's in my head and I can't keep going through this. I don't want to live like this anymore."

"Don't say that," Lucas pressed his forehead to hers. "You don't get to leave me. Not like this. Not by your own hand."

She collapsed into his chest, crying into him as he held the towel tighter.

Down the hall, drills started buzzing. Mason's men moved through the house, their boots crunching on broken glass, hammers banging into frames. Shouts bled through the walls, as guards took position outside. The house was becoming a fortress.

Amelia's voice broke the silence, so faint he almost didn't hear it. "You should let me die."

Lucas froze. His arms locked tighter, squeezing her to him until she gasped. "Don't you dare say that."

Her face lifted, pale and streaked with tears. Her lips shook, but the words still came. "If I was dead, you could live a normal life again. You wouldn't have to bleed for me. You wouldn't have to fight. You could be happy again, Lucas. You could be free."

His jaw trembled. "Happy? Without you? You think I'd crawl back into boardrooms and glass towers while you rotted in the ground? I wouldn't be free without you."

Her sobs cracked into a scream. "Then what am I, Lucas? I'm nothing but weight! I dragged you into this nightmare, and I can't…"

"Stop!" His shout ripped through the room, so sharp even the hammering stopped. His hands clamped around her face, forcing her eyes to his. "You're not weight. You're not broken. You're the only reason I'm still here. You leave me, and I burn the world down."

Her chest heaved, words splintering as her voice shattered. "Why can't you just let me go?"
"Because you're the only thing that's ever kept me alive," he rasped.

They both screamed at each other. Both broken. Both clinging to each other like it was the only rope left in a storm.

Amelia swayed. Her hand pressed to her stomach. A groan slipped her lips.

"Amelia?" Lucas's voice faltered.

Her eyes rolled back. Her knees buckled. She collapsed into his arms, heavy and limp.

"Fuck!" Lucas caught her, laying her onto the bed. The towel stayed dry. No new blood seeped through. Her wrist wasn't the cause this time.

Her skin was clammy, her lips pale and her breathing shallow.

"Mason!" Lucas's roar carried down the hall. Footsteps

thundered up.

He didn't wait. He scooped her into his arms, clutching her close, her head lolling against his shoulder.

Mason appeared in the doorway, face grim. "Lucas…"

"She's burning up." Lucas's voice cracked. "I'm taking her to the hospital. Lock this place down. If Ethan comes near, bury him before I get back."

Mason gave a single nod.

Lucas stormed past, carrying her into the night. Guards stepped aside, silent, as if they knew better than to look him in the eye right now.

The hospital lights burned sterile and cruel. Nurses swarmed the moment they saw the blood-stained towel in his hands, but Lucas refused to let her go until they pried her from his arms. He paced the corridor like a cage animal.

When she woke, she was pale against the sheets. Lucas sat at her side, gripping her hand like a lifeline. His knuckles were white, the towel still crumpled on the chair beside him.

A doctor stood at the foot of the bed, flipping through her chart, voice careful. "Amelia, these cuts on your wrist. Are you feeling suicidal?"

Her gaze flickered to Lucas. His jaw clenched.

"No," she whispered. The lie smooth. She couldn't risk being locked away in a ward. The doctor studied her for a moment longer, then nodded. "We'll respect that. But we're running tests to see why you fainted. We will call you with your blood test results in a few days. In the meantime make sure you get plenty of rest."

Lucas's grip tightened around her hand. His voice rasped. "She's been under stress. That's all."

The doctor didn't argue. He scribbled notes and left them in silence.

He pressed his forehead to hers. "Stay. Please. I can't lose you. Not now. Not after everything. Don't walk away from me…I need you."

Her eyes stung. She turned into him and let the tears come, as the monitor beeped steadily beside them.

Chapter 14

The house was too quiet once Mason's men finished. The windows were whole again, new glass gleaming in their frames, but the smell of plaster dust clung heavy, mixing with the copper tang of dried blood that no amount of scrubbing seemed to lift. Guards shifted outside, shadows passed across the curtains. Every hinge, every lock had been reinforced.

Inside, silence sat like a weight.

Mason broke it first.

"You're losing yourself, he said, voice low. He stood in the kitchen doorway, watching Lucas pace with restless steps. "She needs you steady. Not like this. Not unhinged."

Lucas stilled, his hands braced the counter, shoulders taut. His jaw ticked, eyes shadowed and red-rimmed from nights without sleep.

"You think I don't know what she needs?" His voice was low, dangerous. "I know her better than anyone. She needs to eat. She needs to breathe. She needs to be alive. And I'll carve this city down to ash to make sure she is."

Mason didn't flinch. "She needs a man she can trust, not a warden pacing outside her door."

The words stuck, but Lucas only laughed, a short, harsh sound with no humor in it. He dragged a hand over his jaw, knuckles still raw. "You don't understand obsession. Don't pretend you do."

For a long beat Mason only looked at him, the silence between them heavier than the hammering had been earlier. Then he turned away, leaving Lucas alone with the echo of his own words.

That night, Lucas cooked.

The clutter of pans rang too loud in the silence. Oil hissed. The smell of charred toast and overcooked eggs filled the air. He plated the food, hands shaking only once when he set down the knife he'd been holding too tight.

He carried the tray to Amelia. She sat on the couch wrapped in a blanket, knees drawn up to her chest, her skin pale as porcelain under the dim light.

Lucas set the plate down in front of her and crouched low, his eyes fierce. "You need to eat," he said.

Amelia picked at the food, the fork trembling between her fingers. The first bite turned her stomach. She gagged, covering her mouth, tears pricking her eyes.

"It's okay, try again." His voice soft and caring.

Her head shook. "I can't."

"You can." He moved the plate closer. "You need strength. Amelia, please just try again."

Her tears slipped free. "You don't see it, do you? None of

this matters. It doesn't matter what I eat or how strong I try to be. He'll take me anyway. He always does."

Lucas dropped to his knees, his hands gripping her thighs, eyes burning into hers. His voice cracked, raw. "Don't say that. Don't give him that. Don't you hand him your surrender."

But she only pushed the plate away, sobbing. "Then let me go."

The words carved into him deeper than any blade.

Later, when Lucas shut himself in the office with Mason, Amelia moved.

Bare feet silent on the wood, her body weak but determined. She crept down the hall, hand trailing along the wall to steady herself. Her heart hammered in her throat. Just for air, she told herself. Just a moment away from the walls caving in on her. Maybe if she disappeared, Lucas could breathe again.

Her fingers brushed the door handle.

The door yanked open.

Lucas stood there, chest heaving as if he'd known. "Where are you going?"

Amelia froze, her hand falling from the handle. Tears filled her eyes. "I just.. I just needed…"

He shut the door, leaning in close to her. He forced her chin up to meet his gaze. "You leave this house and he wins. You leave me and I break."

Her lips trembled. "I love you so much I just wanted you free."

Lucas's jaw shook. His voice almost broken. "I'll never be free. Not without you."

Her knees buckled. He caught her before she fell, dragging her against his chest, his arms locked around her.

She trembled in his hold, broken sobs shaking through her.

Fifteen

Chapter 15

The house felt wrong in silence. New glass in the windows, boards screwed into the frames, guards pacing outside. Safe, Lucas told himself. Safer than before.

Inside, he brewed tea for her, set it down untouched. Wrapped her blanket like it could hold the pieces of her together. He sat close enough that his shoulder pressed hers, counting her breaths under the fabric. For a flicker of time it almost looked like peace.

The phone rang.

Amelia snatched it before he could. Her fingers shook as she pressed it to her ear.

"Hello?" Her voice cracked thin.

"Amelia Monroe?" This is Dr. Price," papers shuffled faintly in the background. "I've got your results back from the hospital. It looks like you're pregnant."

The word cut through her like glass.

Her breath stuttered. Her hand flew to her stomach, trembling, and the room tilted. The phone slid from her grip. Lucas caught her under the arms before she collapsed.

"No," she whispered, voice breaking apart. "No, I can't be pregnant. I can't…."

Lucas's eyes burned into hers, sharp with shock. "Pregnant?" His voice was gravel, disbelief threaded with something raw. "You're pregnant?"

Her sob tore free. "I can't, Lucas, I can't bring life into this. Not when he is still out there. He'll take everything. He'll take this too."

He hugged her close to his chest, his mouth against her hair. "He won't touch you. He won't touch what's ours. I'll put him in the ground before he ever lays a hand on you or our child."

She pressed her forehead to his chest, shaking her head. "How do I protect anything when I can't even protect myself?"

"You don't have to," he whispered. "That's mine to do."

The knock came hard. Mason's voice, grim. "Lucas, you need to come out here."

Lucas moved with Amelia still clutched in his arms. He set her gently on the couch and stepped out into the pale morning.

One of the guards lay sprawled on the lawn, eyes glazed, throat cut deep. Blood soaked the grass. A note was stapled to his chest, the paper already spotted red.

YOU CAN'T GUARD WHAT'S ALREADY MINE.

Lucas's teeth ground so hard his jaw shook. Mason stood beside him, silent.

Behind them, the front door creaked. Amelia's hand clutched the frame as she leaned against it, her skin ghost white. Her gaze fixed on the body, and her stomach turned.

She staggered back, one hand pressed to her belly, bile rising sharp in her throat.

"Inside," Lucas barked. He didn't turn, didn't soften. He just wanted to protect her at all costs. "Now."

Mason moved, signalling his men, their boots crunching across gravel as they lifted the body away. The note stayed burned in Lucas's mind.

The phone buzzed again.

Lucas grabbed it this time, but Amelia's hand pressed against his wrist. Her eyes begged. He let her answer.

Her voice shook. "Hello?"

"Sweet Amelia," Ethan's voice slid through, soft and poisonous. "Congratulations."

Her knees nearly gave out. "How do you…?"

"You thought you could hide anything from me?" He laughed low. "I see you gag at the sink. I see the way you cradle your stomach when you think no one's looking. I know you better than you know yourself."

Lucas ripped the phone closer, snarling. "You come near her and I will cut you open so slow…"

"Shhh." Ethan's voice silenced him like a hand over the mouth. "I wasn't speaking to you."

"Don't listen." Lucas hissed against Amelia's hair.

Ethan's tone dropped. "A baby. Precious. Pointless. You think you can build something with him and not with me? I'll bash the brat right out of you myself. Then you'll finally get to work. Night after night, scream after scream. I'll make every drop of you worth the money you owe me."

A sob ripped from her throat. She clutched her stomach like she could shield it with her bare hands.

Lucas's roar cracked the air. "I'll kill you. You hear me? I'll cut your tongue out and feed it to you before I let you touch her again!"

Ethan chuckled, low and giddy. "You can't guard what's already mine."

The line went dead.

The phone clattered against the wall. Lucas crouched in front of Amelia, his hands cupping her face. His voice shaking. "He doesn't get you. He doesn't get this." His palm slid to her belly. "You're mine, Amelia. And so is every breath inside you."

She broke in his arms, sobbing until her voice shredded, the echo of Ethan's laughter still crawling through her bones.

Lucas held her tighter, his voice low and rumbling against her skin. "He dies. I swear it. He dies screaming."

Sixteen

Chapter 16

Sophia came again.

Her face pale, her throat slit, her hands smeared with blood. But this time her fingers were curled around her stomach like she was cradling something that had never been there.

Her mouth opened, her teeth red with blood.

He'll make you bleed like me. He'll take what's inside you too.

Amelia snapped awake with a scream, tears already burning her face. Her whole body jerked, fingers clawing blindly at the sheets as a wave of dizziness crashed through her. Her hand went to her stomach before she could stop it.

Lucas was on her in a second, dragging her into his lap, locking her against his chest. His palm pressed over her belly, holding it like a shield. His voice was low. "Look at me."

She shook her head, eyes glassy. "I can't do this. I'll ruin it. He'll…"

His fingers caught her chin and forced her to meet his eyes.

His jaw trembled. "Don't say that. Don't give him that." His thumb swept her tears. "You don't ruin anything. You're the reason anything good even exists." He pressed her hand harder against her belly. "That's mine to protect. Ours."

A small, broken sound escaped her, barely a breath. Her fingers curled instinctively under his, clinging like she wanted to believe him but didn't know how.

Her sob broke apart. "He always gets to me."

"Yeah," he whispered brushing her cheek. "But I get to you too. And I'm right here."

Her chest cracked. "What if there's not enough of me left to do this?"

He set his forehead against hers. "Then I'll carry it all until you remember how. But you don't get to give up. Not now. Not ever."

She cried into him until she shook. He held her tighter, the weight of his hand on her belly like his hand alone could protect everything she had left.

"I just need to talk to Mason down the hall, okay? I'm not going far. If you need anything. Anything at all, you call out for me. I'll come running."

Downstairs Mason waited, files spread across the table. Grainy photos. Names. Places.

Lucas didn't sit. He leaned over them, his hands braced hard against the table.

"We hit everything tied to him," Lucas said. "Every supplier. Every handler. Every fucking house he's touched. Burn it all."

"You'll bring heat down we can't shake."

"Let them come," Lucas growled. "Obsession is the only reason she's still breathing. He dies. And everyone who ever worked for him dies with him."

Mason studied him for a long, heavy moment. He saw it then, not just the rage, but the fear under Lucas's skin. Fear of losing her. Fear of failing her.

"You're not just going for him," Mason said quietly. "You're going for everything."

Lucas's eyes burned. "I'm going for what's mine. Anyone in the way gets buried."

When he came back to the bedroom, Amelia hadn't moved. She was curled on her side, hand still over her belly, like she didn't trust it to stay there. Her eyes flickered up when he entered.

He climbed onto the bed, and pulled her into him. She came apart against him, trembling, pressing her face to his chest.

"Tell me what you're going to do," she whispered.

"Everything." He said.

"That's not an answer."

"It's the only one I've got." His hand slid over her belly again, holding like he could keep everything inside her safe by force alone. His jaw brushed her hair. "He doesn't touch you. He doesn't touch what's ours. He dies. I'll make sure of it."

She shook until exhaustion dragged her under. When she finally slept, Lucas stayed awake, palm heavy on her belly, breath shaking with the weight of everything he couldn't lose.

He whispered into her hair, low and dangerous. "You'll breathe. You'll see daylight. Both of you. And I'll burn this entire city to ash before I let him take you from me."

Seventeen

Chapter 17

The nightmare dragged Sophia back to her.

Throat split, eyes empty, fingers digging into her own stomach like she was warning Amelia of something unspeakable.

Her dress was torn. Blood soaked the front of it. She held something in her arm, small, fragile. A baby. Its face blurred. Sophia rocked it like a mother, her smile cracked wide across her bruised face.

Then her eyes snapped to Amelia

He'll take this too.

Amelia's scream ripped through the room. She shot upright, breath ragged, tears already burning her cheeks. Her hand flew to her belly, gripping hard, like her body fears it could lose something in the space between dreaming and waking.

The room was dark, the sheets beside her were cold. Too cold. Panic spiked. Lucas wasn't there.

Her pulse rattled, panic clawing her ribs. She dragged

herself to the dresser, yanked the drawer open. The bandage on her wrist itched like fire. Her fingers hooked under the edge, scratching hard. She didn't even realize she was doing it until the gauze peeled back and wetness spread. Blood.

The sting made her gasp. She pressed harder, nails dragging, desperate for an anchor. The floor creaked in the hallway. Her breathing stilled.

"Amelia." Lucas's voice thundered through the doorway.

She froze, her chest seizing. Tears blurred her vision. "I just…" her voice broke. "I just needed it to stop."

He crossed the room in three strides, yanking her hand up. The gauze was smeared, fresh red leaking through where she'd tore it open. Fury and fear collided in his eyes, shaking his whole body.

"You think this saves you?" He pressed his thumb into the wound until she cried out. "You think bleeding makes him stop? All you're doing is handing him another piece of you."

Her sob cracked. "I can't keep it safe. I can't keep anything safe. He'll take it. He'll take me. He'll take everything."

Lucas pressed her gently back against the bed, his body trembling, not with anger, but with fear and need. His hand cupped her jaw, thumb brushing away a tear as his forehead leaned into hers. His voice broke, low and rough.

"Please… just say it baby. I need to hear you say you're mine. He doesn't get to take any part of you, not while I'm here."

Her lips trembled. "I.. I can't."

He squeezed her hand, grounding her, voice barely above a whisper. "You can. I've got you. I'm right here. Just say it."

Tears spilled down her cheeks as she choked out, "I'm yours."

He closed his eyes, a shaky breath rattled from his chest.

"Again, sweetheart."

"I'm yours."

He kissed her, soft and aching like he was trying to stitch her soul back together with his mouth. One hand rested protectively over her belly, his touch trembling with everything he was terrified to lose.

When he pulled back, his voice shook. "You don't get to give up. Not on me. Not on this. Do you hear me? You're mine, Amelia and what's inside you is mine. He doesn't get to touch you. He doesn't get to touch what's ours."

Her sob ripped through her chest. She collapsed into him, blood warm under the bandage, her face buried in his shirt.

"I'm not strong enough," she whispered.

His breath hitched, almost a sob. "Hey, look at me," he lifted her chin, forcing her to meet his eyes. " Then I'll be strong enough for both of us. But you don't get to leave me. Not like this. Not ever."

She shook and shook until exhaustion stole the fight. Lucas stayed, his hand firm on her wrist, his other palm splayed over her belly, like he could hold two lives there by force. He whispered against her hair. "If you bleed, you bleed for me not for him."

Lucas sat her down on the bed, his hand never leaving her wrist. Blood smeared warm across his palm. His jaw clenched hard as he reached for a fresh gauze.

"Stay still," he said, low but commanding. His tone left no room for disobedience.

Her hands shook. " You don't have to."

His eyes cut into hers, dark and burning. "I do. Because you're mine, and I'll always stop the bleeding, Amelia. Always."

The words guttered her. She broke down as he wound the gauze tight, his movement sharp but precise. He tied it off and pressed his thumb against the bandage until her pulse jumped beneath it.

"You feel that?" his voice rough with emotion. "That's proof you're still here. Proof that you're still mine."

Tears ran hot down her cheeks. "What if it doesn't matter? What if the baby only grows inside a nightmare?"

His grip shifted, pressing her bandaged wrist flat against her belly. His other hand covered hers, strong and steady. "Then I burn the nightmare down before it ever touches either of you."

He leaned in until his nose grazed her cheek, breath trembling against her skin. "This life is ours, not his. And he'll never touch it."

Her whole body shook. "I don't want it to end like Sophia."

Lucas's jaw trembled. His hand shot to her chin, forcing her gaze to his. "Listen to me."

His voice shook with the kind of rage only born from love. "You are not her, and you are not a ghost. You're flesh and bone. He doesn't get to steal you into the ground. Not while I'm breathing."

She whispered like it hurt to speak. "I should have saved her. I should've died instead."

He hurled her into his chest, his arms caging her in. His mouth pressed against her hair. "Don't you ever beg forgiveness for living. Don't you ever think your survival was a mistake. Sophia's gone. but you're here. You're mine and I'll make him pay for both of you."

Her body sagged against him, sobs breaking until exhaustion dragged her under. He laid her down and pulled the blanket up over her shoulders. When she finally slept, she whispered Sophia's names, twitching in her dreams.

Lucas didn't sleep. His eyes stayed open, sharp and cold, his voice a low whisper.

"He dies. And when I'm done, not even his ghost will dare whisper your name."

Eighteen

Chapter 18

Morning didn't feel like morning. It felt like the night never ended.

Amelia sat at the edge of the bed, wrapped in one of Lucas's shirts, sleeves swallowing her hands. Lucas knelt in front of her, pressing the bandage one last time like he needed to make sure it held. His thumb lingered on her pulse, slow, deliberate, anchoring.

"Still beating," he muttered. His jaw locked so tight a muscle ticked near his temple.

She nodded, small. "For now."

His hand shot to her chin, forcing her eyes up. "Don't say that." His voice low and rough. "You breathe because I said so. You live because I'm not letting you do anything else. Understand?"

Her throat closed. She nodded again, tears already burning.

He kissed her forehead. For a second it was quiet.

Then a knock came sharp at the front door.

Lucas froze. His knife was in his hand before he crossed the hall. He checked the peephole. Empty.

When he opened the door, the only thing waiting was a box. Cardboard. Ordinary. Wrong

He dragged it inside and dropped it on the table. Amelia hovered in the doorway, her breath already stuttering.

Lucas cut it open with the tip of his blade.

Inside lay a doll.

A baby doll. It's belly was slit open, stuffing spilling out like guts. The dress it wore was white, delicate. A christening gown.

The scent hit next. Sweet. Familiar. Sophia's perfume.

Amelia's scream split the room. Her legs gave and she stumbled back, choking. "No….no …no"

Lucas's hand closed around the doll's neck. He crushed the plastic until it snapped, head rolling across the table. Stuffing scattered like snow. His chest heaved, veins standing out in his neck.

Then the phone inside the box buzzed.

Lucas snatched it up, and put it on speaker, his voice like a snarl. "Where the fuck are you?!"

Ethan's laugh slithered through, low and delighted. "Sweet Amelia."

Her knees buckled. She pressed both hands to her stomach, nails digging through the fabric of Lucas's shirt like she could claw safety into her skin.

"You got my gift," Ethan purred. "A taste of what's coming. I'll bash it out of you myself. Then you'll get to work the way you were suppose to. Night after night. Scream after scream.

Worth every drop."

Amelia sobbed, shaking her head hard. "Stop…Please stop."

His tone sharpened, mocking. "Do you want to know what she sounded like, Amelia? Your precious Sophia? She screamed your name until her throat tore. She begged you to come. And you didn't. You let me carve her open, and she died with *you* on her lips."

Amelia gagged, bile burning her throat. She crumpled to the floor, clutching her stomach, shaking so violently, her teeth rattled. "Stop," she begged, sobbing into her hands. "Please, just stop."

Lucas's roar cracked the air. "I'll rip you apart with my bare hands!" His fist shook around the phone.

Ethan only laughed. "I would love to see you try."

The line went dead.

Lucas hurled the phone against the wall. Plastic shattered, pieces skittering across the floor. His breath came in ragged bursts, his whole body vibrating with fury.

Amelia curled on the floor, arms wrapped around her stomach, rocking and tear streaming down her cheeks.

Sophia's perfume still clung to the air, sickly sweet. It coated her throat, her lungs. She couldn't get it out.

Lucas dropped beside her, dragging her into his lap, pinning her shaking body against his chest. His mouth pressed to her hair. "He dies," he rasped. "I don't care what I have to do. He dies screaming and I'll make him choke on your name before I put him in the ground."

Amelia sobbed harder, whispering through her tears. "I just want it to stop. I just want it to stop."

Lucas's arms crushed her tighter, his palm firm over her

belly. "It will," he promised. "Because I'll stop him. Even if it kills me."

For a long time, he just held her. Her sobs thinned into shivers, then into silence broken by jagged breaths. When she could finally lift her head, her face was blotched red, her eyes glassy and hollow.

Lucas brushed his thumb across her cheek, rough but reverent. "You're not staying on the floor." He crouched and swept her up, carrying her into the lounge room.

He set her down in the armchair by the fire, tucking the blanket tight around her shoulders. A book rested on the table. One she hadn't touched in weeks. He pressed it into her lap, his jaw hard but his voice low. "Read. Keep your head here. Not in his hands. Here."

Her lips trembled. She nodded, clutching the book like it might anchor her.

Lucas straightened, every muscle rigid, his chest heaving with everything he was trying to keep contained. His eyes lingered on her, sharp and raw, then he turned without another word.

The garage door slammed open.

Amelia stared into the firelight, the book heavy in her hands, as the sound of fists hitting leather cracked through the walls. Over and over. Each blow harder, than the last.

In the garage, Lucas's knuckles split open against the punching bag, blood smearing the canvas. His breath tore from him in ragged bursts. Every hit landed with the image of Ethan's face behind it.

"I'll destroy," he snarled between strikes. "I'll tear your world down until there's nothing left. You'll never touch her. Never touch what's mine."

Nineteen

Chapter 19

Morning didn't come softly.

It hit like punishment.

Amelia woke choking, bile already climbing her throat. She stumbled from the bed, bare feet cold against the floorboards, and barely made it to the bathroom, before she fell to her knees. The retching was violent. Her whole body twisting as acid burned the back of her throat.

The door cracked open.

Lucas's voice, rough with sleep and worry. "Amelia?"

She couldn't answer, not between heaves. Her fingers dug into tiles.

He was beside her a second later, wordless. Water ran and then a damp cloth pressed cool to the back of her neck. His hand swept her hair out of her face, his touch steady even as she shook.

When it was over, he eased her back against his chest.

Her breath hitched, weak. "I'm sorry."

"Don't," he wiped her mouth, thumb grazing her cheek. "You don't say sorry for existing."

Her arm fell across her belly, instinctively. "What if I can't do this, Lucas? What if I fail before it even begins? What if I'm already…."

He caught her hand, pressed it flat over his heart. "You won't fail."

Her eyes shimmered. "He knows, Lucas. The doll, the dress…he knows."

He went still. Then quietly, "Yeah. He knows."

Her stomach turned cold. "Then what if he finds us again? What if he gets to me?"

His grip tightened. "He won't. Because I'll kill him before he breathes your name again."

The words weren't loud. They didn't need to be. They vibrated through the air like a promise already carved in blood.

Amelia closed her eyes, leaning into the warmth of his chest. "You sound so sure."

"I have to be," he kissed her temple. "If I stop believing that, he's already won."

She let out a small, broken laugh that sounded more like a sob. "You always make it sound simple."

"Simple doesn't mean easy," he murmured.

When she finally lifted her head, her skin was pale, and slick with sweat. Lucas scooped her up without asking and carried her back to bed. He tucked her under the blanket, adjusted the pillow, and set a glass of water within reach. His movements were sharp, practiced, like this was another battle he refused to lose.

"You need to rest," he said.

"I can't. Every time I close my eyes, he's there."

"Then I'll keep watch."

She reached for his wrist, her fingers trembling. "Promise me you won't leave."

He hesitated. And that hesitation told her everything.

The phone rang breaking the silence.

Lucas stood in one motion, snatched it from the nightstand. "Yeah," he barked. Silence, then a low, dangerous hum in his throat. "Where?"

He listened for another beat, eyes darkening, then hung up.

"What is it?" She asked, voice barely above a whisper.

"Mason's found something. A warehouse. One of the routes Ethan's been using to move the girls."

Her pulse stuttered. "You're going."

"I don't have a choice."

"Then I'm coming."

He turned to her, the command already in his eyes. "You're not coming."

"I won't sit here while you hunt him alone."

"You will," his voice cracked. He pressed a kiss to her temple. "You don't understand, baby. You're carrying everything that's left of me. If something happens to you, there's no me to come back."

Tears slipped free, hot and silent. "What if you don't come back either?"

The knock came before she answered.

Lucas rose and opened the door to Mason and Jase standing on the porch, weapons slung low, eyes alert.

"Mason you stay here," Lucas ordered, his tone leaving no room for argument. "No one gets in. No one touches her.

You see headlights you don't recognize, you shoot before you speak."

Mason frowned. "You're sure about this?"

Lucas's eyes flickered to Amelia. "She's the only thing I've ever been sure about, and you're the only one I trust with her life."

Lucas went back to her, knelt one last time, his hands finding hers beneath the blanket.

"You'll be safe. You have Mason and you have my word."

Her voice broke on a whisper." Lucas…"

He kissed her, slow and deep, a goodbye disguised as a promise. When he pulled back, his lips brushed her ear.

"He dies tonight."

And then he was gone. The door closing behind him.

Amelia sat perfectly still, one hand pressed over her belly, the other gripping the sheet like a lifeline. She didn't realize she was crying until she tasted salt.

"Please," she whispered into the quiet. "Just come back to us."

* * *

The rain came sideways. Lucas didn't slow down.

The black sedan tore through the industrial district, tires spitting water as the docks came into view. The city lights were long gone. Here, everything reeked of rust, rot and the ghosts of men who'd been buried in concrete.

Jase sat in the passenger seat, rifle balanced across his knees. "You sure this is the place?"

"No," Lucas said. "But it will hurt him."

He killed the engine. Silence hit like a heartbeat stopping.

Every instinct in his body screamed *wrong*.

They moved anyway.

The warehouse loomed ahead. Massive, empty, the kind of quiet that didn't feel natural. Lucas's boots crunched on the gravel as he pushed the door open, the metal groaning like it hadn't been touched in years.

"Clear left." Jase murmured.

Lucas scanned right. Crates stacked to the ceiling. Shadows pretending to be still.

His knife slid into his hand out of habit.

They crept deeper. Each breath fogged in the air. The silence pressed heavy, too perfect, too planned.

And then…

Click

A red dot landed square on Jase's chest.

"Down!" Lucas shouted.

The world exploded.

Gunfire tore through the dark. Muzzle flashes strobing through the haze. Splinters rained down as bullets shredded the walls. Jase dove behind a crate, returning fire. Lucas moved faster, low and precise.

He grabbed the nearest shooter, slammed his head into the wall, and drove the knife under his ribs. The man crumpled.

Another appeared behind him. Lucas spun, fired twice. Blood painted the concrete.

But there were too many.

"Fall back!" Jase yelled.

Lucas didn't listen. He moved forward, always forward. Rage burning hotter than pain.

A shot caught him across the side. White-hot agony ripped through his ribs. He hissed, teeth bared, and fired back blind. The bullet took someone's throat out. He didn't even look to see who.

The air stank of blood and gunpowder. Every exhale was smoke. Every inhale hurt.

Somewhere in the chaos, he saw the burner phone. Taped to a pillar, screen glowing.

He reached it, tore it down. The screen lit with one word: **RUN.**

The explosion took out half the building.

Fire bloomed orange and violent, swallowing everything in its path. The blast threw Lucas backward, slamming him into the floor. His ears rang out, vision shattering in and out of focus. The taste of iron filled his mouth.

"Lucas!" Jase's voice cut through the static. "We have to move!"

Lucas staggered up, half-blind. One hand pressed to his bleeding side. The world tilted. He forced it steady. Smoke clawed at his lungs as he stumbled toward the exit.

Bodies burned behind him. Men he'd trained with. Men who'd followed him.

Outside, the rain hissed against the flames.

He collapsed against the hood of the car, breathing in short, sharp bursts. Jase grabbed him, dragging him inside the car before another blast ripped through the building.

As the fire swallowed the skyline behind them, Lucas whispered the only name that mattered.

"Amelia."

Twenty

Chapter 20

The front door hit the wall, the echo shaking dust from the frames. Mason was in the hall, gun raised until he saw the blood.

"Jesus, Lucas!"

"Not now," his voice was shredded. "Where is she?"

"Living room."

Lucas walked in slow, like gravity itself had turned on him. Amelia turned from the fire, her book slipping from her lap the moment she saw him.

"Lucas."

He was soaked, blood smeared his side, shirt torn, soot streaked down his jaw. His eyes found hers like she was the only thing in the world worth crawling home for.

She ran to him. Her arms wrapped around him just as his knees buckled, and they sank to the floor in the hallway.

"You're hurt," she whispered, voice cracked and thin. Her

hands pressed frantically over his ribs, trying to stop the bleeding with nothing but fear and fingers. "Oh my god, Lucas why would you... what happened?"

He cupped the back of her head, his grip tight like he was anchoring himself to her body.

"It was a trap. They knew we were coming. I got out."

"But you're bleeding, your side...." her breath hitched, tears already falling. "You can't Lucas, you can't leave me."

"I won't," he swore, forehead pressing to hers. "I didn't fight through the fire and bullets to die now. I'm here. I'm with you."

Her sob choked into his shoulder.

Footsteps pounded. Mason rounded the corner with the first aid kit, kneeling beside them without a word.

Lucas didn't let go of Amelia, even as Mason sliced his shirt open, blood sticking to the fabric. He only hissed once, jaw grinding shut as antiseptic hit raw skin.

Amelia couldn't stop crying. Her hands shook as she tried to help, pressing gauze where Mason told her, whispering. "You're okay, you're okay." Like if she said it enough, it would become true.

Lucas caught her wrist. "I saw your face in the fire. That's what got me out."

Her throat closed. "Don't say that."

"I mean it," his thumb traced her pulse. "You're why I lived."

He sagged back against the wall as Mason stitched, swearing under his breath.

"Two men stay on the door tonight," Lucas rasped, his voice sharper now. "No one gets near her. No one."

"Already done," Mason muttered. "Ethan's not getting

within a mile of her."

Lucas nodded, then turned his face to Amelia, softer now, more wrecked than she'd even seen him. "Come here."

She crawled into his lap, carefully. Trying not to hurt him. He wrapped his arms around her anyway, like even the pain couldn't stop him from holding her.

"You scared me," she whispered against his neck. "I thought I'd never see you again."

He kissed her temple, then the edge of her mouth. "You'll always see me again. Even if I have to crawl back from the dead."

Her palm drifted down, resting over her belly.

Lucas's hand covered hers. He didn't speak. The look in his eyes said everything: He would burn the world before he let anyone touch her. Or their child.

Twenty-One

Chapter 21

Amelia sat curled on the couch, knees tucked under the blanket Lucas had thrown over her. One hand rested absently on her belly. The nausea wasn't as brutal as it had been the past few days, but it still lingered, low and constant.

Lucas walked in from the kitchen, shirtless. Bruises still forming beneath the fresh bandage that wrapped around his ribs. He held a plate in one hand, two slightly charred slices of toast balanced beside a mug of tea.

"I know it's not fancy," he said, setting it on the coffee table. "But you need to eat something."

Amelia wrinkled her nose. "It smells like you tried to kill the toaster."

He smirked, dropping beside her. "I'm considering it revenge for last night."

She rolled her eyes, but didn't argue. Slowly, she sat up, taking the plate. Her stomach flipped at the first bite, but she made herself chew.

Lucas watched her, like she might fall apart any second.

She hated how much she needed that.

"Is it always like this?" she asked softly. "The sickness?"

He leaned back, arm draped along the back of the couch. "No idea. I've never been pregnant."

Her laugh cracked out of her, short, sharp and real. "Smartass."

But the smile faded quickly. Her hand slid over her stomach. "What if I mess this up?"

Lucas didn't answer right away. He reached over instead, brushing a crumb from her lip. "You won't."

She looked away.

"Amelia." His voice dropped. "You're not in this alone. You've got me. You've got this whole crew ready to kill for you. Hell, Mason threatened to shoot me if I didn't let you rest today."

She smiled faintly. "Mason likes me."

"Mason would carry you around on a velvet pillow if you asked."

She set the toast down and leaned into him, curling into his side. He shifted, pulling her tighter, one hand wrapping over her belly like it was instinct.

"You're doing everything right," he said. "One bite at a time. One morning at a time."

"I don't feel strong."

"You don't have to feel it, to be it."

She closed her eyes, letting his words settle in her bones.

And for a while, they just sat like that. Toast cooling on the plate. Fire crackling low in the background. The war hadn't ended. The threats still loomed. But in hat moment, wrapped in Lucas's arms, Amelia could almost believe they might win anway.

The fire crackled low in the living room, its warmth soft against Amelia's bare legs as she curled deeper into the armchair. Lucas's hoodie hung off one shoulder, the sleeves rolled up just enough to free her hands as she turned the page in her book. She hadn't really been reading, her eyes kept skimming the same paragraph but, it felt good to pretend. To sit in silence and be still for a while.

Lucas paced in the hallway, phone pressed to his ear. "I don't care if he switched burner phones again. Find the signal. If he so much as breathes too close to this house…."

He paused, listening. Tension rolled off him in waves,

Amelia shifted. Her stomach twisted so suddenly it knocked the air of her lungs. The nausea came sharp and fast.

She dropped the book, stumbled to her feet and rushed down the hall.

Lucas's voice trailed after her. "Amelia?"

She didn't answer.

He was already moving, dropping the phone to the hallway table. "Amelia!"

He found her on her knees, curled over the toilet, arms trembling as she retched again and again. Her hair stuck to her cheeks, her body shuddering with each wave.

He dropped beside her, pulling her hair back, steadying her with one arm around her shoulders. "I've got you," he murmured. "Breathe. Just breathe, baby."

She coughed, gasped. One shaking hand drifted to her belly, pressing there like she was trying to shield what little she could. Her lip wobbled. She didn't speak, but her silence said enough.

Lucas's chest cracked wide open.

"I know," he whispered, kissing the side of her head. "I know you're scared. But you're not alone. Not for one second."

She turned into him ,damp cheek against his chest, her fingers curling into the fabric of his shirt.

His hand found her stomach, covering hers. Steady. Anchoring.

"He doesn't get near you. He doesn't get near either of you."

She nodded once, almost to small to see.

He tilted her chin gently. wiped beneath her eyes with his thumb. "Let me take care of you. Let me fight for you."

A tear fell down her cheek.

"I'll keep you safe," he promised, forehead resting against hers. "Even if it kills me."

Lucas pressed his lips to her temple, his voice gravel-soft. "C'mon, let's get this taste out of your mouth." He reached over and turned the water on, wetting a washcloth before holding it to her lips.

She wiped slowly, still trembling, and leaned into his touch, like it was the only thing tethering her.

"I feel disgusting," she murmured.

"You're carrying a life," he said. "You're a goddamn goddess." her eyes flooded. "It's just morning sickness."

"I know." his hand drifted over her back. "Still doesn't mean you don't deserve to be looked after."

He didn't rush her. He stayed there, crouched on the cold bathroom floor like it was the only place in the world he needed to be.

When her shaking finally eased, he kissed the top of her head and moved toward the tub. Turning the taps and checking the temperature twice.

"I'm running you a bath," he said quietly. "You need to feel warm again."

She didn't argue.

When he came back to her, he helped her up with a hand under her arm, careful and steady.

Steam filled the bathroom as he guided her to sit on the edge of the tub. He knelt again, pulled off her hoodie, then kissed her shoulder. His touch lingered, reverent. No rush, just grounding."

"Let me take care of you," he murmured.

Amelia blinked fast, tears catching in her lashes. "I hate feeling like this."

"I know," he said. " But I'd rather hold your hair while you puke every hour than have you go through this alone."

Her hand curled around his wrist, anchoring there. His other palm drifted to her belly, thumb brushing in slow circles.

The bath was ready.

Lucas stood, helping her in gently. Once she was submerged, he knelt beside the tub again, rolling his sleeves. He washed her arms and shoulders, silent and steady.

By the time the bathwater cooled, Amelia's skin was soft with heat and exhaustion. Her eyelids drooped. Her head lolled back against the edge of the tub.

Lucas dried her slowly. He wrapped her in one of his shirts, the fabric loose and warm, then lifted her into his arms.

She curled against his chest, arms tucked between them.

"I can walk," she mumbled.

His grip only tightened. "Don't care."

He carried her into the bedroom, the light already low. He laid her down gently, then knelt to pull the blankets up, tucking them right around her like a promise.

Her hand caught his as he started to pull away.

"Stay," she whispered, voice raw from nausea and everything else she couldn't name.

Lucas didn't hesitate. He sat on the edge of the bed, then shifted to lay beside her. One arm wrapped around her waist, the other resting protectively over the curve of her belly. His forehead pressed to hers.

She exhaled shakily.

"I've got you." he murmured into her ear.

She didn't respond. But her hand stayed clutched in his shirt until her breath slowed and she finally slipped into sleep.

He waited. Counted every heartbeat and watched the way her lashes fluttered, the crease between her brows softening as she sank deeper.

Then he eased himself out of bed, silent as a shadow.

The phone on the dresser was already blinking.

One missed call.

Blocked number.

His blood turned to ice. Lucas slipped from the room, shutting the door without a sound.

Downstairs, the second burner buzzed again.

He picked up.

Didn't say a word. On the other end, a voice hissed like static and sin.

"Closer than you think."

Lucas's jaw locked. "If you so much as look at her..."

"You should check the cameras, lover boy."

The line went dead.

Lucas sprinted to the control panel hidden behind the bookshelf, his fingers flying over the keys.

The outer perimeter flickered to life.

Motion detected. Northeast tree line.

A shadow. Tall and lurking inside the edge of the property. Then gone.

He stared at the screen, breath caught halfway in his chest.

Ethan had been here.

Watching and waiting.

Lucas's hands curled into fists at his sides, shaking with the effort not to rip the monitor off the wall.

Down the hall, Amelia slept. Soft, peaceful and unaware.

And Lucas knew, this war was only beginning.

Chapter 22

Lucas sat in the dim security room, screens humming softly in the dark. He hadn't slept. He couldn't. Not after the warehouse. Not with the knowledge that Ethan was still breathing somewhere out in the city.

He scrubbed a hand down his face, leaned forward and replayed the motion alerts from the night before.

Bedroom feed.

Amelia curled in Lucas's hoodie, one hand on her stomach. Peaceful. Soft. Breathing without pain. The only light in the entire fucking world.

He hit play.

The footage flickered. A glitch. A jump. Two seconds lost, and then a shadow appeared at the foot of her bed.

Lucas froze.

The figure moved closer, slow and deliberate as if savoring each step. A man, shoulders broad, head tilted slightly as he stared down at Amelia.

Lucas's chest went tight enough to crack.

He slammed his hand against the desk. "No! No! No!"

The man reached out and brushed Amelia's hair off her cheek.

Lucas saw red. Darkness crowded the edges of his vision.

The feed showed Ethan bending down, his face inches from hers. His lips moved. Whispering.

Lucas's fist shook violently.

Then Ethan's hand drifted lower. To her stomach. To the curve of their child.

His fingers splayed there, almost gentle.

Lucas shoved his chair back so hard it slammed the wall. "I swear to God!"

He replayed the clip, again and again. His pulse beat in his throat.

Then he noticed it.

A shift in pixelation. A frame distortion. The timestamp stuttering.

Not natural. Not an error.

"Motherfucker."

He replayed the clip in slow motion, and there is was barely half a second long:

A different bed.

A different angle.

A different blanket.

The room wasn't theirs. Ethan had filmed himself somewhere else, with a bed staged to look like hers, blanket the same colour, lighting the same shade.

Then he hacked the feed. Spliced the footage, timed it

perfectly with a blackout.

Lucas's blood iced. Ethan hadn't been in their house but he had still stood over something pretending to be Amelia, whispering promises over a fake belly, touching a fake version of her like a ritual.

And that was worse. So much fucking worse.

"He wants me to think he was here," Lucas breathed, voice trembling with fury. "He wants me to lose control."

The burner phone buzzed on the desk.

Lucas answered without breathing. "I'm going to cut your throat open."

Ethan laughed softly. "Relax, lover boy. I didn't touch her. *Not yet.* But you saw how easy it could be."

Lucas's free hand dented the edge of the desk.

"You're not untouchable," Ethan whispered. "And neither is she."

The line went dead.

Lucas sprinted down the hall, lunge on fire, breath shuddering in his throat.

He burst into the bedroom.

Amelia stirred at the sound. "Lucas…?"

He was at her side in a heartbeat. Hands on her face forehead pressed to hers, breath shaking. "You're safe. You're okay. I've got you."

"Wh…what happened?" She whispered.

He shook his head. "Nothing. You're hear that's all that matters."

He couldn't tell her. Not this. Not what he saw.

Lucas pulled her into his lap, held her so tight she squeaked. His hands flattened protectively over her belly.

She tucked her face into his neck, breathing slow. Peaceful.

He felt the moment her body softened, the tiny exhale that meant sleep had taken her again.

He kissed her temple, swallowing the tremor in his chest.

* * *

It was just after 7 a.m. when the house was surrounded.

Boots hit the ground hard. Radios crackled. Men moving through the trees like shadows with orders. And Lucas stood in the middle of the front lawn, fists locked at his sides, jaw tight enough to crack bone.

Mason strode across the grass, rifle resting against his shoulder.

"You sure?" he asked.

Lucas didn't blink. "I saw it."

Mason hesitated. "You sure it was actually?"

"Yes!" Lucas snapped, eyes sharp enough to cut. "The footage showed him standing over her bed. Whispering to her. Touching her." His voice shook once, barely. "Touching her stomach."

Mason swore under his breath, face darkening. "Christ."

Lucas dragged in a breath, chest rising and falling like it hurt. "Five-minute blackout, A corrupted file spliced into the feed. He hacked our system, Mason. He didn't get in…" His voice cracked with fury. "But he wanted me to think he did."

Mason's expression hardened immediately. "So none of it was real?"

"Oh, it was real enough," Lucas growled. "He chose that

angle. Chose that room. Chose her. He wanted me to see him over her." His teeth clenched, jaw trembling with rage. "He wants me unstable. He wants me off balance."
Mason nodded slowly. "Psychological warfare."

"He's already in the house," Lucas said, voice low. "All he had to do was get inside the cameras."

Mason turned toward the men. "Double perimeter. No gaps. Full rotations. I want someone watching every feed, every second. If he tried this shit again, I want eyes on it."

The house behind Lucas suddenly felt like a shell.

Vulnerable. Breached, even if not physically.

Mason lowered his voice. "And Amelia? You gonna tell her?"

Lucas's gaze snapped toward the window where she slept. "No."

His voice was iron. "She thinks she's safe here and she needs to keep believing that."

Mason watched him carefully, then nodded once. "Then we keep it quiet."

Lucas's jaw flexed. "We don't let him inside her head."

* * *

The sheets were still warm when Amelia stirred, tangled in the soft cotton of Lucas's hoodie. The scent of him wrapping around her like a second blanket.

Her hand was curled over her stomach, a habit now. But this time...

She froze.

Movement. A flutter. Then pressure and then again. Not cramps. Not nausea.

Just a tiny kick.

"Oh," she breathed, eyes going wide.

Her palm pressed flat against the swell of her belly, her heart slamming against her ribs. It was real. *So real.* The first real proof that someone was alive inside of her.

Tears pricked her eyes, a flood of emotion swelling too fast to name.

A laugh caught in her throat, choked by the sob already climbing up. "You're really there," she whispered. "You're okay."

She looked to her side, already turning to wake Lucas…

But he wasn't there.

His side of the bed was cold now. The blanket tossed back. No footsteps. No sound.

The joy in her chest faltered.

She sat up slowly, hand still cradling her stomach. "Lucas?"

Silence.

She swung her legs over the edge of the bed, heartbeat ticking louder with every second.

The floor was cold against her bare feet. She padded down the hallway, listening.

Nothing.

Not the hum of the coffee machine. Not the murmur of a voice. No Mason. No footsteps.

No front door opening.

The house felt too still.

"Lucas?"

Still no answer.

The kick came again, stronger this time and she stumbled, one hand catching the wall, the other splaying over her stomach. Her breath hitched.

She steadied herself, heart drumming, instinct begging her to find Lucas.

She moved toward the front of the house, drawn by the faint murmur of voices outside.

Then the screen door creaked open. Her hair was still tousled from sleep, eyes soft. She didn't hear what they said but the way they suddenly went quiet, the way both men shifted like they were caught....she noticed that.

"Morning," she called gently.

Lucas turned too fast. "You're up early."

"I couldn't sleep," she said. "The baby moved."

Mason's brow lifted in surprise, but he said nothing, giving Lucas a small nod before stepping away to give them space.

Lucas met her halfway across the lawn. "You felt the baby kick?"

She smiled, tired, raw but real. "Just a flutter. But it felt like something good. Like we're still here. Still alive."

Lucas's expression cracked. He wrapped his arms around he before she finished the sentence, his hand spreading over her stomach.

"You're not going anywhere," he murmured. "Neither of you are."

Amelia leaned into him. "Promise?"

He kissed the side of her head. "I swear it."

Behind them, Mason watched with a haunted look in his eyes.

Twenty-Three

Chapter 23

Ethan sat in the dark, the only light coming from the multiple monitors flickering in front of him. Static lines rolled down the screen every few seconds. The system fighting his intrusion, but he only smiled at the interference.

"Hello, dove," he whispered, leaning closer.

Amelia slept on the middle screen, curled on her side, one hand tucked beneath her cheek, the other resting protectively over the curve of her stomach. Lucas's hoodie hung loose around her shoulders.

Beautiful.

Breakable.

His.

He adjusted the feed, sharpening the image until he could count each breath she took.

Lucas thought cameras protected her. He didn't understand that cameras were *invitations*.

"Still pretending you're safe," Ethan murmured, brushing his thumb across the monitor like he was stroking her cheek. "Still pretending you can erase me."

Her hair spilled across the pillow like a dark halo. She twitched in her sleep, just enough to make his pulse kick.

Fear lived in her bones. He'd planted it there himself.

"And look at you now," he hummed, eyes drifting lower, to the gentle rise beneath the blanket. "Growing something you think will save you."

His smile cracked. "That thing isn't a blessing,' he whispered. "It's a shackle. It's weakness. It's him."

His fingers tapped the monitor, right over where her belly rested.

"I should've crushed it out of you when I had the chance."

Amelia shifted, her hand tightening subconsciously over her belly.

Ethan swallowed, breath hitching. He leaned in even closer, lips grazing the cold glass of the screen.

"Oh you feel me, don't you?" his voice dipped into something sick and twisted. "Even in you sleep. Even through the walls. Through the cameras. you know who owns your breath."

A small ripple of movement flared beneath the blanket.

The baby kicked.

Ethan laughed, a shuddering, broken sound only madness could make.

He pressed his palm flat to the monitor like he could feel it through the pixels.

"That's right," he whispered. "You know who's watching. You know who she belongs to."

His gaze dragged to her wrist, where a sliver of bandage peeked from under the sleeve.

He zoomed in.

Slow.

Hungry.

"You still wear me," he breathed. "Right under your skin. Every mark is a prayer. Every cut is you saying my name."

For a moment, he just watched her sleep, his expression softening into something almost tender if not for the violence simmering beneath it.

He placed two fingers against the screen, a mockery of a caress.

"Sleep while you can, little dove," he murmured. "Soon you'll wake up remembering exactly who made you."

He leaned back in his chair, shadows cutting sharp across his face as he whispered:

"I'll see you soon."

Then he clicked off the feed.

* * *

The air in the warehouse stank of rust, rot and regret.

Rows of girls lined the walls. All branded property before they even knew how to scream. But none of them were her.

Ethan moved like a shadow through the space, one hand trailing across the concrete wall, the other adjusting the camera feed now fixed on *her* house.

He hadn't touched her the way he'd planned. Not properly. Not *enough*. She got out too early, ripped from his system before he could perfect her. Before she leaned to kneel on command. Before she bled for him the way she was meant to.

"you were supposed to be my prize, Amelia," he whispered dragging smoke into his lungs like it might keep him calm. "I fed you. Clothed you. Broke your bones just right and you *ran* before I could finish."

He flicked the cigarette into a puddle and watched it hiss.

His men were packing a delivery van across the lot. Another shipment. More girls.

"She was going to make me millions," he muttered to himself, pacing now. "But she wasn't just about the money, no…she was my art. My *masterpiece*. I was saving her for the highest bidders. After I had my fun."

"You were supposed to be my prize, Amelia," he whispered, dragging smoke into his lungs like it might keep him calm. "I fed you. Clothed you. Broke your bones just right. And you *ran* before I could finish."

His fingers twitched like they missed the feel of her throat.

He stopped in front of a chair bolted to the floor. Leather restraints dangled from the arms. The metal under the seat was stained dark.

"I had a name for her," his voice dipped. "The dove. I was going to paint it on her collar."

He turned, eyes burning toward the monitor.

Amelia slept in a bed that wasn't his, beside a man who didn't deserve to breathe.

Lucas.

A growl curled through Ethan;s chest.

"She looks softer now. Domestic," his lips curled. "Doesn't suit her."

He tapped the screen, the image zooming on her swollen

belly. His eyes lit up, not with joy, but with something crueler. Hungrier.

"You think that baby's going to save you?" His voice turned evil. "You think he'll protect you? He's already failing."

He stepped back, chest rising and falling too fast. Then he called out "Pack the black van. I want it spotless. No blood this time, not yet."

One of the men froze. "We movin' them girls tonight?"

Ethan didn't even look at him. "No. We're preparing for *her.*"

The man hesitated. "You sure she's…"

Ethan turned and one look silenced him

"Amelia was mine before Lucas even knew how to spell her name. I trained her bones to snap on cue. I branded her in places no one else has touched."

He pointed to the monitor.

"That's not a mother," he said, venom low in his throat. "That's a disobedient pet with a collar that doesn't match."

He cracked his neck, then smiled.

"Two more nights. I want her home by the full moon."

Then, softer. Sicker. A whisper meant only for her:

"Let him keep holding her while he can. Soon, she'll be back where she belongs. On her knees, In chains. Carrying my name on her tongue or not at all."

Chapter 24

The radiologist smiled softly. "That's your baby's heartbeat."

Amelia's eyes flooded. The sound hit her like a storm breaking through her ribs. "It's so fast."

"That's how it's supposed to be," the woman said. "Strong heartbeat, perfect rhythm."

Lucas exhaled, a shaky sound that almost wasn't a laugh. "That's my girl."

Amelia blinked at him, a small smile trembling through her tears. "You think it's a girl?"

"I know it," he murmured, brushing her knuckles with his thumb. "She's got that stubborn heartbeat. Just like her mother."

The radiologist chuckled. "Would you like to know for sure?"

Amelia nodded. "Please."

The wand moved again. The screen shimmered, blurred

and then sharpened. Small feet, curved spine, a tiny flick of movement.

"There she is,' the woman said gently. "A healthy baby girl."

Amelia covered her mouth, a broken sound escaping her. Lucas pressed his forehead to hers, his voice barely a whisper.

"You hear that?" he murmured. "Our girl."

Her hand pressed over his. "She's really real."

"She's everything," he said simply.

He kissed her temple, tasting salt and hope. For one breath, the world felt whole. The fear receded, just long enough for them to believe in something fragile.

They left the clinic with a single ultrasound photo, and a silence that felt warm instead of heavy. Lucas drove with one hand on the wheel and the other resting on her thigh. She traced the picture with her thumb, memorizing the curve of their daughter's form.

"Have you thought about names?" she asked quietly.

He smirked. "You've had a list since the second you felt her kick."

She laughed through the sniffle. "Maybe."

"Then tell me."

"Not yet," she whispered. "When it feels right."

The peace ended at the front door.

Lucas stiffened the moment he turned the key. He felt it first. The way the air in the house felt wrong.

"Stay behind me," he said quietly.

There was a small box on the hallway table. No label. No fingerprints. Just placed.

He picked it up and slit the tape with his knife.

Inside was a stuffed rabbit. Cream-coloured. The exact one

Amelia had stopped to look at in the store days ago.

Tied around its neck was a tag.

Two nights. Sleep well. She'll look just like you. -E.

Amelia's breath broke. "Lucas…" her hand went to her belly instinctively. "He knows. He knows she's a girl."

He grabbed the note, voice shaking with fury.

"Mason!"

Mason appeared from the hall within seconds.

Lucas's voice was gravel. "Find out how this go in here. Check the feeds. All of them."

Amelia's voice trembled. "How does he know, Lucas? You said we were safe."

He hesitated.

"Tell me," she demanded, sharper this time, fear cracking the edges.

His jaw flexed.

"I found something a few days ago. On the security feed."

Her stomach dropped. "What?"

"A five-minute gap. And a new file spliced in during the blackout."

Her knees went weak. "What was on it?"

Lucas swallowed hard. "It was you. Your room. Your bed. Except…" He dragged a hand through his hair, breath unsteady.

"Except it wasn't real. He filmed a fake setup. You blanket, your pillow and hacked it in."

Amelia's hand flew to her mouth.

The room tilted.

"He faked being inside the house?" she whispered.

"He wanted me to believe he stood over you," Lucas rasped. "Wanted me to see him brushing your hair. Whispering to your stomach. Touching what's ours."

A choked sob tore out of her chest.

"He…he pretended to be near our baby."

Lucas stepped closer, voice low and raw.

"I didn't tell you because I didn't want you to break. But him sending this note? The timing. It means he's escalating."

Her body shook. "He's already inside Lucas. Not the house… me. He's always inside, in my head. In my dreams. I can feel him."

Lucas cupped her face in both hands, forcing her to meet his eyes.

"Look at me. He cannot touch you. Not in this house. Not in this world."

Tears streaked down her cheeks.

"Then why doesn't it feel safe?"

He pressed his palm over her belly, protective, desperate.

"She's safe with me." His voice cracked. "You both are."

The silence that followed was broken by Mason's voice from the hall. "He's been in our systems again. The timestamp lines up. He's watching the cameras."

Lucas turned, rage flickering cold in his eyes. "Then we shut him out."

Amelia's breath came too fast. The walls felt closer. Every inhale scraped like glass.

Her hands flew to her stomach, trembling uncontrollably.

"If he can walk into our house while w're gone, and leave a toy meant for *her,* what stops him from coming back when we are asleep? When I'm alone? When I can't even run?"

Lucas looked took her hands gently in his. "Hey. Look at me. Breathe."

But she couldn't. The air was too thin, her chest too tight. "He's already won. He's everywhere, in everything. I cant..."

"Amelia," his voice dropped low, steady. The tone that used to bring her back from nightmares. He crouched in front of her, forcing her to meet his eyes. "You're safe right now. He's not here."

Her voice broke. "you can't promise that."

"I can," he said. "Because I'll die before I let him near you again."

Tears spilled down her cheeks. "You said that before, and he still found us."

Lucas's jaw clenched, pain flickering across his features. "Then I'll bury him deep enough this time he won't crawl out."

Amelia tried to stand, but her knees gave out. Her body folded, breath ragged. "I can't do this. I can't keep fighting him. Sophia. The nightmares. The baby..."

"Don't," he said softly, catching her before she hit the floor. "Don't talk about her like she's part of the pain. She's the light that came out of it."

Her hand gripped his shirt. "what if I ruin her? What if I can't protect her?"

A high, thin ringing filled her ears, drowning out Lucas's voice. The hallway wavered. Her fingers went numb. Then everything went black.

"Amelia!" Lucas caught her, shaking her lightly, his voice raw. "Hey, hey...open your eyes."

Mason burst into the hallway, gun in hand. "What happened?"

"She's out. Pale as a ghost." Lucas lowered her onto the couch, brushing her hair from her face. "Come on, baby.

You're fine. I've got you."

Mason crouched beside him. "She breathing?"

"Yea, but it's faint. She hasn't eaten. She's sick, stressed to hell." His voice cracked. "She's killing herself trying to stay strong."

Lucas's tone turned lethal. "Lock this house down. Two men outside her door. One on every window. You see anything that moves, you don't wait to confirm…drop it."

Mason nodded and started barking orders.

Lucas pressed a damp towel to Amelia's forehead. Her lashes fluttered.

"Hey," he whispered, relief breaking through his voice. "There you are."

She blinked up at him, confused and small. "What happened?"

"You fainted," his palm moved over her belly, gently. "Scared me half to death."

Her voice trembled. "I don't want to lose her."

"You won't," his jaw tightened. "Not while I'm breathing."

Her eyes filled again. "I don't know if I can do this."

He leaned in close, voice low and fierce. "Then I'll carry it for both of you. You don't have to do anything but breathe."

Tears slipped down her temples. "I'm tired of being scared."

His thumb brushed her lips. "Then let me be scared for you."

Mason appeared again in the doorway. "House is secure. No one's getting in."

Lucas didn't look up, his focus was locked on Amelia. "Good. Keep it that way. We don't sleep until this ends."

Lucas brushed a tear from her cheek. "You're shaking. you need to lie down in bed."

"I can't," she breathed. "If I close my eyes…"

"You won't be alone," his voice softened even further. "Come on. Let me take you."

He slid an arm around her waist, and guided her toward the bedroom, slow and steady. Never letting her stumble. Her legs felt weak beneath her, her breath came shallow and uneven.

When they reached the bed, he lifted the blanket and helped her ease down onto the mattress. She curled instinctively on her side, one hand over her belly, the other gripping his wrist like she'd drown if she let go.

He brushed her hair back, voice low. "You rest." leaning close enough that his breath warmed her temple. "I'll make sure no one touches you. No one touches her."

Her grip loosened as the weight of exhaustion pulled her down. Her eyelids drifted, fluttering. Her body softened under his touch, breath coming slower and deeper.

"I'm right here," he whispered.

Her fingers slipped from his wrist as sleep finally claimed her.

* * *

The room was dark.

Too dark.

Too still.

Amelia ran. Her bare feet hit the floorboards of a hallway that never ended. Doors stretched on forever, locked, nailed shut, bleeding around the hinges.

A baby cried. Somewhere close. Somewhere she couldn't reach.

Then the crying stopped.

Ethan stepped out of the darkness.

A knife in one hand. A stuffed bunny in the other.

Her womb pulsed like it could feel the threat.

"She's mine now," he whispered. "Just like you were."

Amelia screamed.

Her body jerked up in bed, a choked cry tearing from her throat. Sweat drenched her skin and tangled her hair against her cheek.

And then…

"Shh, I got you."

Lucas was already there. Crouched beside the bed, one hand gripping hers, the other stroking her damp hair back from her face. His voice low, steady but sharp at the edges like he was barely holding it together.

"It was just a dream, baby. You're safe. You're with me."

Amelia's lips trembled. "He…he had her." Her hand curled protectively around her belly.

"She was crying and I couldn't get to her. He said…he said she was his."

He sat beside her, pulling her into his lap. "She's not his. She's ours and I will kill him before he ever gets close."

Amelia buried her face in his chest, clinging to the fabric of his shirt like it was the only thing keeping her grounded. Her whole body shook.

She looked up, glassy-eyed. "You haven't slept."

"I won't. Not until he's in the ground. Not until she's safe. Not until you can close your eyes without flinching."

Tears slid down her cheeks, but she didn't wipe them away.

Lucas tucked her tighter into his chest, rocking slightly. "It's almost morning. Just rest a little longer."

"I can't."

"Then let me hold you through it."

They sat like that for what felt like forever. Her trembling slowly easing, his heartbeat a steady anchor against the chaos still swirling inside her.

When she finally fell into a light, uneasy sleep against his chest, Lucas didn't move.

He stayed wide awake. Eyes trained on the shadows.

Finger resting on the trigger.

Twenty-Five

Chapter 25

The phone buzzed. Mason's name lit the screen.

"Mason?"

"Lucas, it's confirmed. He's moving tonight. Ethan's coming for her."

Lucas's hand tightened on the phone. "Then we'll be ready."

"Lock it down," Mason said. "Every door, every window. No one blinks."

The call ended.

Amelia's pulse thundered. "Lucas, what was that?"

He pocketed the phone too fast. "Nothing."

"Don't lie to me," she whispered. "I know that look."

His eyes softened for a fraction of a second before guilt hardened them again.

"He's coming," she said, the words more breath than sound. "Tonight."

Lucas didn't answer. That silence was all the confirmation she needed.

Her chest tightened. "You said we were safe here…"

"We are," he said, too sharp, then gentled his tone immediately. "We are, Amelia. I swear it."

But she was already shaking her head, pacing, her breath coming too fast. "He always gets to me. No matter where we go, no matter what you do."

Pain hit without warning. A sharp, twisting cramp ripped through her stomach.

"Lucas…"

He was on her before she hit the floor, catching her as she doubled over, gasping.

"Breathe, baby. Look at me. Breathe."

Her voice came out strangled. "It hurts. Oh god, it hurts."

He scooped her up and carried her to the bed, hands trembling even as he tried to steady her.

"You're okay. I've got you. I've got you."

"Lucas… what if something's wrong with the baby?"

His throat worked, his voice hoarse. "I'm calling the doctor. Just hold on."

The next ten minutes blurred. Her breath came in sobs, his words were the only thing anchoring her. Then, the front door opened. The doctor arrived. A middle aged woman with tired eyes and the kind of calm that comes from seeing too much.

"Let's get you lying down, Amelia."Her voice was soft but firm. "Deep breaths for me, sweetheart."

Lucas hovered near the bed like a storm contained.

Doctor Riley pressed a stethoscope to her chest, then to her stomach. "Pain started how long ago?"

"Ten minutes," Lucas said before Amelia could answer.

"Any bleeding?"

She shook her head weakly. "Just…pressure."

The doctor nodded, moving efficiently but carefully. She checked her blood pressure, the cuff hissing tight around her arm. Her brows furrowed slightly.

"Blood pressure's high. You're under extreme stress." She turned to Lucas. "She needs absolute rest. No adrenaline. No confrontation. No fear. Her body's reacting to everything she's holding in."

Lucas's jaw flexed. "That's not an option. Not with him coming."

"Then make it one," the doctor snapped quietly. "Because if she keeps going like this, she won't make it through the night without complications. She and that baby need peace, not promises."

Lucas's throat bobbed. "Do whatever you have to. Keep my girls safe."

The doctor's tone softened as she turned back to Amelia. "The cramps should ease, but your body is telling you it's at its limit. I'm giving you something mild for the pain, but the real danger isn't physical. It's the stress. You need to rest, Amelia. No more arguing, no more pacing, no more fear. Let him handle the rest."

Tears spilled down her cheeks. "I'm trying," she whispered. "I really am."

The doctor brushed her arm gently. "Then that's enough for now."

Lucas sat on the edge of the bed, reaching for her hand. His thumb stroked the inside of her wrist, over the faint scars that never faded. "You hear that? You rest. That's your only job tonight."

She nodded, trembling. "Lucas, I'm scared."

"I know," his voice cracked. "But you're not alone in it."

The doctor finished her notes quietly, glancing once more at Lucas. "Keep her laying flat. Hydrate her. If the pain returns or she starts bleeding, call me immediately. And for God's sake, keep her calm."

When the door closed behind her, the house went quiet again.

Lucas stayed beside her, fingers still laced with hers, watching the steady rise and fall of her chest until he could finally exhale.

He bent low, pressing a kiss to her forehead. "He won't touch you," he murmured. Amelia lay on her side, propped against a mound of pillows, one hand protectively over her stomach. The cramps had dulled, but the fear hadn't.

For a while, she listened to Lucas's footsteps fade down the hall, the muffled sounds of running water in the kitchen, cupboards opening and closing. The house was still, every sound amplified by the hush that had settled over them. A minute later Lucas came in quietly, a glass of water in one hand, a pill in the other. He sat on the edge of the bed.

"Small sips," he said gently, handing her the glass. "And take this. It'll keep the pain from creeping back."

Amelia obeyed, her fingers trembling slightly as she brought the glass to her lips. When she was done, she set it on the nightstand and leaned her head back against the pillow.

Lucas reached out and brushed a loose strand of hair from

her face, his thumb lingering at her temple. "How's the pain?"

"Bearable," she murmured. "But I can't stop thinking about tonight."

His jaw tightened, but he didn't pull away. "You don't need to think about that. you just need to rest."

Her hand curled around her bump. "He wants to take this from me, Lucas. He wants to rip everything good from me again."

Lucas's voice dropped, soft but steel-edged. "He's not getting close. Not this time. Not ever again."

There was a knock, soft but deliberate. Lucas stood, crossing the room in two strides and cracking the door open. Mason stepped inside, his usual edge softened.

"How is she?" he asked, eyes scanning the room.

"She's okay. Doctor said rest, fluids, and zero stress," Lucas said. "We're doing what we can."

Amelia pushed herself up a little, offering a tired smile. "Mason."

He gave her a nod, then crossed to the side of the bed and crouched so they were eye-level. "We've got eyes on every approach. Front gate, woods, the old service road. Trip wires, motion sensors, men on shifts. No one's getting in without going through us."

Amelia's throat tightened. "I don't want anyone else to die because of me."

Mason's expression didn't flinch. "You let us worry about that. You just focus on keeping that little heartbeat safe."

She looked down at her belly, the shape of it barely noticeable beneath the blanket, but already everything to her. "He won't stop."

"No," Lucas agreed. "But neither will we."

Mason stood, glancing at Lucas. "I'll double the watch around the perimeter as the sun goes down. Radio checks every fifteen minutes. Snipers on the east line."

Lucas nodded. "I want floodlights on all corners. And if even a shadow moves, I want to know about it."

Mason looked back at Amelia one last time. "You're not alone in this, Amelia. None of us are leaving your side."

She blinked fast, her voice breaking. "Thank you."

When he was gone, Lucas returned to her side, kneeling so his face was close to hers.

"You're safe," he said again, gentler this time. "We've built a wall around you. All you have to do is stay behind it."

Her lip quivered. "Promise me you won't go too far."

He brushed his lips over the back of her hand. "I'll also be close enough to hear your heartbeat."

She cradled her belly tighter. "She's mine. This baby is mine. Ethan doesn't get to touch her. Not even in his nightmares."

Lucas's eyes darkened, and pressed his forehead to hers. "Not even then."

Twenty-Six

Chapter 26

For the first time all day, Amelia had finally fallen asleep. Her breaths slow and shallow, her hand curled protectively around her belly. Lucas stood in the doorway and watched her for a moment longer than he should've, his heart pounding like it already knew what was coming.

He didn't want to leave her. But he had a war to win before it ever reached her feet.

Lucas stepped out into the hall and headed for the back of the house, where the real work was happening. As the door to the sun room creaked open, cold air and tension hit him in the chest.

Mason was hunched over the map laid across the table, cigarette hanging from his lips. Around him, a half-dozen men stood with weapons slung and radios clipped to their vests.

"Status?" Lucas asked, voice low and controlled.

Mason looked up, eyes hard. "Perimeter trip wires are live. Spotters are posted at the treeline. Rooftop's got Clay and Jase, both with scopes. North and west are weak points. Too much open ground. If Ethan sends his dogs through there, we'll know, but it'll get loud."

Lucas folded his arms, scanning the grid. "Let it get loud. I want them to choke on it."

Mason smirked grimly. "We're baiting the devil tonight."

Lucas met his eyes. "Then let's drown him in holy water."

He stepped closer, running a finger along the map's lines, calculating, always calculating.

"We hold the house. No matter what. If they get through the first line, fall back and funnel them here. They don't touch the house. They don't get a fucking glimpse of her."

Mason nodded. "We've got guards on rotation inside, too. One at the front, one in the hall, one by the basement entrance."

"And if they breach before I call it?"

"Shoot to kill."

Lucas's jaw flexed. "Good."

There was a beat of silence before Mason added, "you sure she's ready for this?"

Lucas looked toward the hallway, toward the room she was sleeping in.

"No," he said. "But I am."

A breeze kicked through the cracked window, rustling the edge of the map.

Lucas straightened, his voice colder now. "Tonight, we stop running."

Mason crushed the cigarette under his boot. "Then let's make it biblical."

The sky outside the windows was stained dark violet. The last blush of daylight swallowed by the night.

Amelia stirred beneath the soft weight of the blankets, her lashes fluttering as the remnants of uneasy dreams clung to her ribs. Her body still ached, but the cramps had dulled, and the silence told her Lucas must've kept his promise. No one had come for her yet.

She sat up slowly, her muscles stiff, her hand drifting instinctively to the soft swell of her belly. The baby kicked, a tiny thud against her palm, and she exhaled, lips parting in a breath of something like relief.

Grabbing the nearest blanket, she wrapped it around herself and padded out into the hall, her bare feet whispering against the floorboards.

The house was quiet. Not peaceful. It was tense and bracing.

She found him in the lounge, standing near the window. Lucas had one hand resting on the sill, the other holding a half-empty glass of water. He was staring out into the dark like he was trying to see the future. When he turned and saw her, something in his face softened.

"Hey," he murmured, crossing the room to meet her. "How are you feeling?"

"A bit better," she said honestly. Her voice was still hoarse with sleep. "Still tired."

Lucas reached out, brushing his knuckles down her cheek. "You scared me earlier."

Before either of them could say more, a sharp crackle interrupted the quiet.

"Movement on the east perimeter," a voice came through the radio clipped to Lucas's hip.

It was Clay, one of the rooftop spotters. "Just past the treeline. I count two shadows. No ID yet."

Lucas's expression turned to stone. He pulled the radio free. "Eyes on. Don't engage unless they cross."

Amelia's stomach flipped. "Lucas…"

He was already moving. "Come on," his hand slid into hers, firm, steady but fast.

"Is it him?"

"I don't know yet," he said, guiding her quickly down the hall. "Could be scouts. Could be nothing. But I'm not taking the fucking chance."

He ushered her back into the bedroom and turned to her. "Stay in here. Do not open this door unless it's me."

"Lucas…"

"I mean it Amelia," his eyes burned. "No matter what you hear. No matter what happens. You stay right here."

Amelia clutched the blanket tighter, her heart pounding. "What if..?"

"You won't be alone. There's a man at the end of the hall and I'll be back before you can miss me."

She nodded, but tears clung to the edges of her lashes.

Lucas stepped forward and kissed her, not soft this time. Fierce. Like he was trying to memorize her. Like this might be the last chance.

Then he pulled back, whispered, "I love you" and slipped out the door.

The click of the lock echoed like a gunshot.

Amelia stood there, wrapped in a blanket, her baby kicking beneath her palm, staring at the door as the night swallowed them whole.

Outside, the world was bracing for violence.

Inside, she was bracing for heartbreak.

She backed away slowly, the blanket trailing behind her, and lowered herself onto the bed.

The sheets still smelled like Lucas. She curled onto her side and placed her palm over her belly.

Another tiny kick.

Still there. Still alive.

Still hers.

Her lip trembled.

"Hey, baby girl," she whispered, her voice breaking on the words. "It's just you and me right now."

She let her fingers trace the soft curve of her belly, anchoring herself with every movement. The only thing keeping her from unraveling completely was the thud of tiny feet against her hand.

"I don't know what's going to happen tonight," she said softly. "I wish I could promise you the world. Safety. A life without monsters. but right now…all I can promise is that I'm going to fight like hell to keep you safe."

Her throat closed, and she swallowed a sob.

"I didn't think I'd get to be your mum. Not after everything. But somehow…somehow you're here. And you're real."

The room was dim. Just the flicker of the bedside lamp, like a heartbeat. Like hope refusing to die.

"Your daddy's out there being brave for both of us. And I know you don't know what that means yet but you'll understand someday. He's the kind of man who would burn the world just to keep us warm."

Another kick. This one stronger. Almost defiant.

Amelia let out a choked laugh. "You're a fighter, huh? Just

like him."

She paused, her smile fading as she stared at the door again.

"If anything happens to me, I want you to remember this okay? You were always wanted. Always loved. Even before I saw your face. " She rubbed her belly gently. "If you ever feel lost, know that every beat of my heart, every fight in my bones, was for you. Even when I was scared."

Her voice cracked. "And if you ever wonder who you got your fire from…it wasn't just him. It was me too. Because loving you gave me something I never had before. A reason to survive."

Outside, there was a muffled thud. Maybe a gunshot. Maybe thunder. Maybe death come knocking early.

Amelia flinched, her hand tightening protectively over her belly.

Her heartbeat kicked hard against her ribs. Then came another sound, closer this time. The sharp crack of glass, the low rumble of men shouting over each other.

Her pulse spiked.

That wasn't thunder.

The first shots rang out with no warning, rapid, violent, ripping the night apart. The house shook with it. Somewhere down the hall, someone screamed, followed by the heavy slam of a door and the crunch of boots over gravel.

She jerked upright. "Lucas?" Her voice was barely air, too fragile to reach past the walls.

The next volley of shots answered for him.

Her body moved before her mind could catch up. She stumbled to the bedside table, yanked open the drawer. Inside lay the gun Lucas had shown her how to use, once in case of emergency.

This was one.

Her hands trembled as she wrapped them around the cold steel. It felt heavier than she remembered.

"Come one, come on…" she whispered to herself, flicking the safety off, just like he'd taught her.

A crash split the air, she spun toward the door, heart battering against her ribs so hard it hurt.

The baby shifted beneath her hand, one sharp, terrified flutter.

"I know, I know," she whispered to herself, tears streaking hot down her face. "Mummy's got you. I've got you."

She scanned the room, looking for anywhere safer, anywhere she could see the door but still hide. Her gaze landed on the space beside the tall chest of drawers across the room.

Small enough to fit behind.

She squeezed into the space beside the tall dresser, back pressed to the wall, every muscle wound tight.

The sounds down the hall were chaos. Shouting, more gunfire, the dull thud of a body hitting wood.

She tried not to imagine whose.

Her knuckles whitened around the gun. She whispered to the dark, voice trembling but fierce. "You don't touch us. You don't take us again."

Footsteps stopped. A pause. Long enough to make her heart stop.

Then the doorknob turned, slow.

Amelia's fingers hovered on the trigger, breath snagging in her throat. The latch clicked open, and the door creaked inward. Slow, deliberate, taunting.

A man stepped inside.

Not Lucas.

He was tall, broad-shouldered, his clothes dark and slick with rain...or blood. His smile spread slow when his eyes found her crouched in the corner, the gun trembling in her hands.

"Well, well." He smirked, shutting the door behind him with a click. "Didn't think I'd get this close without catching a bullet first."

Amelia didn't move.

He took a few steps closer, his boots whispering against the floor. "Boss is eager to get you back, sweetheart." His gaze dropped to her stomach, cruel amusement twisting his mouth. "Wonder if he'll let you keep that thing inside you, or cut it out before it starts crying."

Her stomach turned to ice.

"Stop talking," she whispered, but he only laughed. A low, ugly sound that made her skin crawl.

"Maybe he'll let you keep it long enough to remember what love felt like," he said, tilting his head. "Then he'll take it away just to remind you who you belong to."

Her hand steadied. The shaking didn't stop but the aim did.

"Don't," she whispered again. "Don't say another word."

He took another step, hands raised in mock surrender. "Easy now, mama. Wouldn't want to hurt..."

The gun went off.

The sound tore through the room, deafening and final.

He dropped before the rest of his words could leave his mouth. A bloom of red spread across his chest, stark and fast, soaking the carpet. His body hit the floor with a dull, heavy thud that made her flinch.

For a moment there was nothing.

No sound.

No breath.

Then the gun slipped from her shaking hands. She pressed herself back against the wall, tears spilling as the ringing in her ears faded.

Her stomach ached, fear and adrenaline. But she couldn't look away from him.

She'd never kill anyone before.

Not like this.

Not to protect.

Her lips trembled. "I told you not to talk."

The door burst open.

Lucas filled the frame, gun raised until he saw the man on the floor. His chest heaved once, before his eyes found her, small and shaking in the corner.

"Amelia," he breathed, holstering his weapon before dropping to his knees beside her.

Her hands were still trembling when he cupped her face, forcing her eyes up. "Did he touch you?"

She shook her head, tears falling faster. "No. I….he was going to…."

"I know," his voice cracked like it hurt to speak. "You did what you had to."

"I killed him Lucas."

He glanced at the body, then back at her. "Good."

Her breath hitched.

"He would've taken you," Lucas said, his voice low, shaking with barely contained rage. "He would've taken both of you. You stopped him."

She broke then, sobs shaking through her body. He caught her, dragging her against his chest, cradling her like she might shatter.

His heartbeat was a thunderclap against her ear. "He'll never touch you. Never."

Her fingers fisted in his shirt, clinging like she was drowning. "He said Ethan's coming for me...he said..."

"I know," Lucas said, his hand sliding protectively over her stomach. "I'll be waiting for him when he does."

He pressed his lips to her temple before standing, and helping her up.

Mason appeared at the doorway behind him, blood spattered across his sleeve. He looked at the body and then at Lucas.

Lucas didn't look away from Amelia when he spoke.

"Clean it up. Then lock this house down."

* * *

The gun still lay where it had fallen.

The body was gone, dragged away by Mason's men. But the blood on the carpet hadn't dried yet.

Lucas crouched in the hallway, cleaning the edge of his blade in silence, his face unreadable in the flickering light. Behind him, Mason whispered into his radio, his voice sharp and controlled.

"West line held. One breach. The rest backed off once shots were fired."

Lucas stood. "how many?"

"Five, maybe six total," Mason replied. "Just a scout team.

136

Probably meant to test our response time. One pushed too far." He jerked his head toward the bedroom. "You think he knew she'd be the one to pull the trigger?"

Lucas's jaw ticked. "Doesn't matter. He found out too late."

They stood in silence for a moment, then Mason clapped Lucas on the shoulder.

"Whatever Ethan's planning next, it's not happening tonight. Our perimeter's solid, and our men are posted every ten feet. He won't get close without bleeding for it."

Lucas nodded once. "Stay sharp. Double the guards at both ends. I want eyes on everything until sunrise."

Mason gave a low whistle to the men outside and disappeared into the night, barking orders.

Lucas turned back toward the bedroom.

When he opened the door, he found her sitting on the edge of the bed, blanket draped over her shoulders like a fragile barrier. Her knees were tucked in, eyes closed, lips moving silently as if she was saying a prayer.

"Amelia."

She flinched at the sound of his voice, her eyes snapping open. For a second, panic flashed there, but then she saw him, really saw him and her shoulders slumped.

"He's gone," Lucas said gently. "They're all gone. At least for tonight."

She nodded slowly, her hands moving instinctively to her stomach.

"I didn't know I could do that," she whispered. "Pull the trigger."

"You did what you had to do," he said. "You saved both your lives."

He crossed the room, sitting beside her, reaching out and

pulling her into his arms.

Her body melted into his. "I don't feel safe her anymore."

"You're safest here. With me. With our men. But if we need to move…"

She shook her head quickly. "No. I'm just scared. For her. I keep thinking what if I froze, what if I'd missed…"

"But you didn't," Lucas said, tipping her chin up to meet his gaze. "You didn't freeze. You fought like hell. Like a mother who would die to keep her baby safe."

Her throat tightened, and she buried her face into his shoulder. "She deserves better than this."

"She'll get better than this," He pulled back and pressed his forehead to hers. "Because we're going to survive this. All three of us."

Her lips quivered. "He'll come harder next time, won't he?"

Lucas nodded slowly. "Yes. But so will we."

Twenty-Seven

Chapter 27

The morning sun bled pale light through the curtains, casting long, soft beams across the bedroom floor.

Amelia stirred in the bed, her limbs aching like she'd run a marathon in her sleep. Her first breath was shallow. Careful.

She wasn't sure if it was from fear or fatigue.

Lucas was still beside her this time. Not in the bed, but sitting in the corner chair, the same black pistol resting across his thigh like a warning. His eyes were red-rimmed from no sleep.

A knock tapped gently at the door. Lucas stood, gun in hand.

"It's Dr. Riley," came a muffled voice.

Lucas unlocked the door without a word. The doctor stepped inside, dark curls pinned back, medical bag in hand. Her eyes flickered instantly to Amelia.

"You've had quite the night," she murmured, her voice calm

but firm. " Let's take a look at you and the baby."

Amelia sat up slowly, blanket draped over her lap, her hands cradling her belly.

"I'm okay," she whispered.

Lucas didn't move far. He stood by the window, watching the woods.

"Let me be the judge of that," Dr. Riley said gently, slipping a blood pressure cuff around Amelia's arm. "Pulse is elevated. That's no surprise. But I need you to breathe for me, alright?"

Amelia nodded and inhaled shakily.

"Any more cramping?" Dr. Riley asked, palpating her lower abdomen with clinical care.

"Some dull ones…but nothing like last night," she whispered.

"Good. Heartbeat's still strong. She's a fighter, this one."

Tears filled Amelia's eyes, but she blinked them back.

"Your blood pressure's high," the doctor continued. "Understandable, considering. But we need to bring it down. Stress like this is dangerous for both of you."

"I'm trying," Amelia said softly. "I really am."

Lucas finally turned, his voice rough. "What else does she need?"

"Rest. Hydration. No adrenaline. No more running and no more panicking. If her blood pressure spikes again, she could go into early labor."

He nodded grimly. "Understood."

"I'll leave something to help calm her nerves if it gets bad," Dr. Riley said, gathering her things. "But the real prescription is safety and quiet."

Lucas walked her to the door, speaking low. When he came back, Amelia reached for his hand."

"She said she's a fighter," she whispered.

Lucas knelt beside her again. "So is her mama."

He pressed a kiss to her stomach, then another to her lips. "You just rest. I'll keep the monsters at bay."

The hallway was thick with tension, but quieter than it had been in days. Lucas moved through it like a ghost. Quiet, watchful, lethal.

Down the hall, Mason and three others stood by the front windows, still in gear, weapons slung. They hadn't slept either.

"Any movement?" Lucas asked.

"Just shadows," Mason muttered. "Wolves won't come in daylight. But they will come again."

Lucas nodded, jaw tight. "I need you to run into town. Get the prescription Dr, Riley left. If her blood pressure spikes again, I'm not risking it."

Mason hesitated. "You sure you want me to leave?"

"You'll be back before nightfall. And you're the only one I trust not to fuck it up."

That was all it took. Mason grabbed his keys.

Lucas watched the door close behind him, then exhaled slowly and turned toward the kitchen.

He cracked eggs, sliced toast. Everything precise. Quiet. When he plated the food, he added a tiny rosebud he found in a glass next to the sink, something soft in the middle of all this ruin.

The bedroom was warm and dim when Lucas returned. Amelia was propped up against the pillow, her blanket tucked under her arms, one hand resting on her belly.

"You're spoiling me," she said softly, eyeing the plate.

Lucas set the tray on her lap. "Don't get used to it. I don't cook for just anyone."

Her lips curved. "So, I'm not just anyone?"

He leaned down and kissed her forehead. "Not even close." She took a bite, chewing slowly. "I think she's getting bigger," she whispered after a moment. "Everyday, It's like…I'm sharing more of me. I feel her more now. She's kicking stronger."

Lucas sat beside her. His palm gently came to rest over her belly.

Then…

Kick.

A jolt under his hand.. Firm and real.

His eyes snapped to hers. "Was that?"

Amelia smiled through her tears. " Yeah. That was her."

For the first time in days, Lucas's expression cracked open. Something raw. Awe and terror and love all tangled in his eyes.

"She's real," he murmured. "She's really in there."

"And she already knows her daddy." Amelia whispered.

Lucas didn't speak. He couldn't. He just leaned down and pressed his forehead to her belly, breathing her in like a prayer.

Amelia smiled softly, leaning her head against his shoulder. They stayed like that for a long moment, the room wrapped in warmth and the steady rhythm of her breathing.

Then, quietly, she said. "I keep thinking about names."

Lucas look down at her, "Yeah?"

"Just… when everything's quiet like this, I think about who she's going to be." Amelia smiled faintly. "I thought of the name Ivy. It feels strong but soft. Like vines through concrete."

Lucas let the name settle between them. "Ivy," he repeated. "I like it."

"You do?"

He nodded, brushing his knuckles down her cheek. "It sounds like someone who survives. Someone who grows in the darkest places."

Amelia blinked against the sting in her eyes. "That's all I want for her."

Lucas leaned in, his lips brushing her temple. "She already has that in her. She's yours."

Amelia reached for his hand again, guiding it back to her belly. A flutter. A soft, gently nudge against his palm.

"She's saying hi," Amelia whispered.

Lucas grinned, one of the rare, raw ones that only ever came out when it was just her. "Or letting us know she likes her name."

They both laughed softly, leaning into each other.

For a little while, there was no Ethan. No guns. No threats. Just Ivy. Just the promise of a future still holding on, still growing, no matter how many storms tried to rip it from them.

* * *

A soft knock came at the door.

Lucas shifted slightly, careful not to wake Amelia as he eased off the bed and padded across the room. He opened the door just enough to see Mason standing there, a brown paper bad in hand and dark circles carved beneath his eyes.

"She okay?" Mason asked quietly.

Lucas nodded. "She's resting."

Mason handed over the bag. "Pharmacy opened early. I got

the doctor's script filled. Painkillers, prenatal vitamins and something to help keep her calm."

Lucas took the bag, their hands brushing for a second. "Thanks, brother."

Mason's gaze slid past him toward the room. "She's strong. After last night...what she did..."

"I know," Lucas said. His voice hoarse with emotion. "But she shouldn't have had to be."

Mason gave a small nod and stepped back. " We've got the perimeter locked down. No one's getting close without bleeding for it."

Lucas didn't reply. He just nodded once and closed the door softly behind him.

He returned to the bed and knelt beside Amelia, brushing her hair back gently. Her eyes fluttered open at his touch, lashes heavy.

"Hey," she whispered.

"Mason got your medicine. Want to try taking some now?"

Amelia nodded, struggling to sit up. Lucas helped her with a hand at her back, guiding the pills to her palm, and holding the water to her lips.

The medicine went down with a wince, and she leaned into him afterward, her head finding his shoulder, like a muscle memory.

"I hate this part," she whispered.

"I know."

"I feel so weak."

Lucas wrapped an arm around her waist and pulled her closer. "You're not weak, baby. You're still here. That's everything."

She didn't respond, but he felt the soft catch of her breath, the way her body finally began to loosen. Her hand drifted back to her belly, fingers splaying protectively. Lucas cover it with his own, his thumb tracing light circles across the think fabric of her shirt.

"Ivy's kicking," he murmured. "That's her way of telling you she's okay."

A faint smile ghosted over Amelia's lips as he eyes drifted shut. "She's probably braver than I am."

Lucas leaned in, pressing a kiss to her temple. "She's yours. Of course she is."

Amelia's breathing evened out, her body finally surrendering to the pull of rest. Lucas adjusted the blankets around her and eased onto the bed bedside her, cradling her gently to his chest.

He stayed awake, long after her breathing deepened. One hand on her back. The other over her belly. Guarding two heartbeat with his own.

As the sun broke through the curtains, casting soft golden light across the room, he closed his eyes, but only for a moment.

Because night would come again.

And so would Ethan.

Twenty-Eight

Chapter 28

"She killed him," Ethan said, calm as glass before it shatters. "My fucking man. Dropped him like trash on her bedroom floor.

He wasn't pacing. That would imply agitation. No, Ethan moved like something coiled, slow, precise, the kind of calm that only came before carnage.

"She used the gun Lucas gave her. Isn't that romantic?" His voice dipped into a mockery of sweetness, a cruel grin twitching at his mouth. "She's learning how to protect what's *his*. Not what's *mine*."

He spat the last word like poison and slammed his fist into the wall. The crack echoes through the safe house, silencing the room of armed men. One of them twitched, smart enough not to flinch too hard.

"She was awake. Shaking. I saw it in her eyes," Ethan whispered. "She knew. She *felt* me coming. My girl always

146

did have instincts."

He turned, gaze burning. "And what did you do? You failed. One fucking job, slip past the perimeter, grab her while she was soft and scared. But no. You got cocky. Smiled at her. Talked."

His boots thudded across the floor, slow and deadly. He stopped in front of the youngest one, a guy no older then twenty.

"What did he say to her?" Ethan murmured. "Right before she painted the fucking walls with his brain?"

The guy swallowed. "Something about the baby. Just…a joke, boss."

Ethan smiled. A real one this time. The kind that didn't belong on a human face.

"Oh," he said softly. "A joke."

Then, without warning, he pulled his gun and shot the kid in the foot. The scream rang out sharp. Blood sprayed across the floor.

"Next one who jokes about my *girl*, I'll take the tongue first. Understand?"

A chorus of shaken nods followed.

He lit a cigarette, breath steady despite the chaos.

"She was never supposed to get this far," he said, more to himself now. "I was going to start her slow. Break her in, ease her into the life. She would've been my best product. My *favourite.*"

A long exhale of smoke. "But now she's got this fantasy, that she can be *safe.* That she can have *love* and a *baby* and a life that doesn't end under my thumb."

He turned, eyes like shards of obsidian.

"So here's what we do. Next time, we go bigger. I want Lucas and every one of those little solders dead before they even hear us coming. We burn the walls down."

"And her?" One of the older men asked.

Ethan grinned.

"She walks through the ashes barefoot, bleeding, and straight back into my arms. Where she belongs."

He crushed the cigarette under his heel and looked out the boarded window toward the distant hills.

"She'll learn. They all do."

He turned and stood in front of the table, watching the flame from a single candle flicker across the map spread before him. The layout of Lucas's estate, marked in red.

X on the bedroom.

A bloody thumbprint on the nursery.

"I should've killed her that night in the basement," he murmured. "Before she started thinking for herself. Before she learned the sound of her own voice."

His fingers curled around a silver necklace on the table, her old one. The one she wore when she was his. Still smelled like her skin.

He pressed it to his lips.

"She *thinks* she's free."

He paced again, hands twitching with the need to destroy something soft.

"You think hiding behind security and rifles makes her safe?" He hissed, as if Lucas could hear him. "You think putting a baby in her erases me?"

His laughter was hollow, dead behind the eyes.

"She was *mine* before she bled. Before she screamed. Before she ever dared to dream of someone else's arms."

Behind him, one of the older men approached carefully, like he was nearing a wild animal. "Boss…we got movement. Might be one of Mason's runners. Should we take him alive?"

Ethan tilted his head. "No. Kill him. Burn what he carries."

"But.."

Ethan turned slowly, and the look in his eyes shut the man up before he finished the sentence.

"I don't want *messages*," Ethan snarled. "I want *funeral pyres*. I want Amelia to look out the window and see smoke. Smell it in the air while she cradles that parasite in her belly. I want her to know what it costs to try and run."

He walked back to the map, tracing a line from the perimeter to her bedroom window.

Then, quieter, more intimate. "She'll come back to me. She always does."

He reached into the drawer beside the map and pulled out the baby onesie he's stolen from the store. Pale pink. Tiny. He ran it between his fingers like a relic.

"Let her name the baby if she wants. Pick something pretty. I'll carve it into the headstone myself."

Twenty-Nine

Chapter 29

The light through the windows was pale gold when Amelia stirred again.

She blinked slowly, feeling the weight of safety before memory caught up. Lucas's arms were still around her. One draped over her waist, the other curved under her shoulder, hand curled gently over her belly, like he was anchoring them both to this moment.

His eyes were open.

"You didn't sleep," she whispered, her voice rough.

"I didn't want to," he said, voice low, as if speaking louder might break something fragile.

"Didn't want to miss a second of this."

Her lips twitched. "Of watching me drool on your arm?"

"Of watching you breathe," he corrected. "That's all I need."

She turned a little, hand drifting to his chest. The soft thud of his heart was steady beneath her fingers. And when she looked up, there was something raw in his eyes.

Something unspoken.

"What is it?" She asked.

Lucas didn't answer right away. His throat moved, like he was trying to swallow down a truth too heavy to speak.

"I've been scared before," he said, finally "Guns in my face. Blood on my hands. That kind of fear, I could handle. But this?" His hand flattened gently over her stomach. "You. Her. I'm fucking terrified."

Her eyes stung. "You don't have to be strong all the time, you know."

"Yeah, I do," he said, voice almost breaking. "Because if I fall apart, who's going to protect you?"

Lucas froze, then slowly moved his hand to her bump. They both waited. A moment later, there. A firm thump under his palm.

"Ivy," he whispered. "She's getting stronger."

"You think she'll have your eyes?"

He smiled, the kind that didn't quite reach his eyes. "God, I hope not. Yours are trouble enough."

A laughed slipped out of her, too real, too needed.

He leaned his forehead against hers. "I want to kiss you so bad it hurts."

She let out a breath that shook. "Then kiss me."

Lucas hesitated. Just a heartbeat. Then his lips found hers, soft and slow. His hands moved up to cradle the back of her neck, holding her like she might slip away if he wasn't careful.

Amelia kissed him deeper. Fingers curled into his shirt. Her body remembered him. Trusted him.

But when she shifted, Lucas pulled back slightly, breath catching.

"We should be careful," he murmured against her lips.

Amelia nodded. "I know."

His forehead pressed to hers again. "Doesn't mean I don't want you."

"Wanting you doesn't scare me," she whispered. "Losing you does."

His eyes burned.

He kissed her again, slower this time, more deliberate. Like a promise written in touch. Like the world was ending, and this was the last thing he wanted to remember.

When they finally pulled apart, her cheeks were wet again, but not from fear this time.

Lucas smiled, just a little. "You always cry when I kiss you?"

"Only when it feels like home."

They sat there for a while, just the three of them, letting the silence stretch around them like a safe house made of breath and heartbeat and love they didn't know how to name yet.

Then came the knock.

Lucas tensed instantly, every muscle in his body snapping tight as a wire. He pulled away from her gently, kissed her temple, then grabbed the gun off the nightstand.

Amelia sat up, blanket clutched to her chest.

At the door stood Mason. His face was pale, jaw clenched. He held something wrapped in a clear evidence bag, gloves on his hands.

Lucas's voice turned to steel. "What the fuck is that?"

Mason didn't speak. Just held the bag out.

Inside it was soft, pink and soaked with dried blood.

A baby blanket.

Amelia's stomach dropped. Her vision went tunnel-black

for a second.

"No.." her hands trembled.

Lucas didn't blink. Didn't breathe. Just stared at the blood-stained fabric like it was the trigger to the part of him he kept buried.

"There was note," Mason said tightly. "Typed. Said, '*Still think you can keep her from me? Tick, Tock.*'"

Lucas didn't move for a long moment. Then he turned, slow and dangerous, and handed the blanket back to Mason like it burned his skin.

"Get this out of here."

Mason nodded and disappeared down the hall.

Lucas turned back to Amelia, who was already crying silently, her arms wrapped around her bump like she could shield Ivy with skin and bone alone.

"I'm not strong enough," she whispered.

"You're stronger than any of us," Lucas said, sitting beside her, pulling her into his arms again. "But you don't have to fight this alone."

She buried her face in his neck, and Lucas held her like he was holding both mother and child.

"We're going to end him," he whispered. "And when we do, I'm going to burn every piece of him that ever touched your life."

* * *

Lucas had told her to rest. Begged her, really. But Amelia couldn't stay still.

She paced the length of the hallway barefoot, her fingers dragging along the wall like she needed something to tether

her to the moment. The silence wasn't comforting. It was heavy. Too heavy.

Her hand found her bump. Ivy moved beneath her skin like she knew her mother's heart was breaking all over again.

"Shh, baby," she whispered. "Mama's okay. you're safe. I promise."

But the words tasted like lies.

Lucas caught her standing there a while later. "Amelia. Come lie down. Please."

She didn't argue. Just let him lead her back to their room and tug the blanket over her. He kissed her forehead and tucked her close.

"I'll be right outside," he said. "The second you need me."

She closed her eyes.

Sleep came slowly but it didn't come gently. It dragged her down like chains around her ankles.

In the dream, there was blood on the floor again.

The hallway was too long, the walls warping like heat waves. Every step sounded wrong. The air buzzed with something beyond hearing.

And then she saw her.

Sophia.

Sitting on the old swing the way Amelia had found her, head tilted, hair hanging in wet, stringy clumps, feet bare and streaked with dirt. The rope creaked softly even without wind.

Her eyes...

God, her eyes.

Open. Glassy. Staring straight into Amelia as if death hadn't dimmed her at all.

"I didn't think you'd come back here," Sophia whispered, voice thin as a dying breath.

Amelia's knees nearly buckled. "Soph…"

"You didn't come for me." Not angry. Not accusing. Just a fact delivered like a blade.

Amelia shook her head hard. "I didn't know, Soph…I didn't know what he was doing to you. I swear."

Sophia's head tilted, water dripping from her hair, hitting the dirt like raindrops. "You knew something was wrong."

"I was trying to survive," Amelia choked out. "I couldn't save myself, how was I supposed to save you?"

Sophia stepped close. The swing swayed behind her, empty again.

"You survived," she whispered. "And I didn't."

Amelia's chest split open. "I would've come for you. You were my best friend."

Sophia blinked slowly. "He made sure you didn't."

A breath, cold as winter ghosted over Amelia's skin.

"You lived," she whispered. "And I didn't."

Tears burned down Amelia's cheeks.

"I would've traded places with you," she said. "A thousand times."

Sophia reached up. Not to hit. Not to hurt.

Just to brush a knuckle down Amelia's face.

"But you didn't."

Then she was gone.

Amelia shot upright in bed, gasping.

Her chest heaved. The scream had already torn from her throat, but it felt like it was still stuck there, clawing at her ribs. Cold sweat soaked her skin. The room was dark, but sharp around the edges, like shadows were watching.

Lucas jolted awake beside her. "Amelia?"

She didn't answer. Couldn't.

Her breath came fast, too fast. Tight and shallow, her hands pressed to her face, then her chest, then her stomach as if she had to check she was still whole.

"Breathe," Lucas said, voice gentle. "You're okay. You're safe."

She threw the covers off and stood, pacing the room like a caged animal. Her footsteps were near silent but frantic, her arms wrapped around herself as though she could hold her insides together.

She didn't speak.

Didn't cry.

Just breathed like she couldn't get enough air, like the dream still had a fist around her throat.

Lucas rose slowly, staying back, watching her move in jagged lines across the floor.

"You're safe," he said again. "Whatever you saw, it's not real. You're here. With me."

She shook her head.

Her shoulders trembled. Her hands curled into fists at her sides. Her body was vibrating with something unspoken, like guilt made flesh, rattling her bones from the inside out.

Lucas stepped closer.

"Talk to me, baby. Please."

Amelia turned slowly, her face pale.

"Sophia." Her voice cracked. Just the one word. But it gutted him.

She sank to the edge of the bed, eyes wide and unfocused, staring through the walls like the dream was still bleeding into the room.

"I haven't had a dream about her in a little while," she

whispered. "I thought they were gone."

Lucas lowered beside her, his hands hovering like he didn't want to scare her off.

"She died because of me," Amelia said. "She died, and I keep living like I deserve to."

"You *do* deserve to," Lucas said softly. "You didn't kill her, Ethan did. And you have every right to keep breathing."

Her chin quivered.

He placed a hand over hers, grounding her.

"You need to look after yourself for Ivy," he said, voice rough. "For me. For Sophia, too. Because you survived and you still get to love her."

Amelia's breath hitched again.

Too fast. Too shallow. Too loud in the quiet.

She pressed a shaking hand to her chest, then dragged it down to her stomach like she needed proof she was still real. Her pulse pounded so hard it felt like it was rattling her ribs.

Lucas moved closer, his voice steady but cracked at the edges.

"Amelia, look at me. You're okay."

But she wasn't. Her skin crawled. Her vision narrowed until all she saw was the ghost of Sophia's blood, seeping into the corners of her mind. The sound of her voice, the one that had begged, *Please, don't let him take me.*

It was everywhere.

In the walls. In her pulse. In her bones.

Her nails dug into her palms until the sting cut through the noise. She didn't notice at first that she'd drawn blood.

Lucas did.

"Amelia," he said softly, stepping in front of her. His eyes flicked to her hands. "Hey… hey stop. Don't do that."

She froze, caught in the sound of his voice but not quiet hearing him.

Her body trembled.

He reached out slowly, wrapping his hand around hers, prying her fingers open one by one. Red marks bloomed across her skin.

"Breathe with me," he whispered. His voice broke. "Don't go back there. Not like this."

Her breaths came faster instead, ragged and wet, her chest heaving as she shook her head. "I can't, Lucas… I can't do this again."

"Yes, you can," he said, his thumb tracing over her knuckles, grounding her. "You already are."

She was spiraling too fast to believe him. The edges of the room blurred. Her throat closed. Her body was betraying her again, sweat cold, heart screaming.

She wanted to crawl out of her skin.

Then…

A kick.

Sharp and sudden, right beneath her palm.

Amelia gasped, freezing mid-panic, her eyes darting down to her belly.

Lucas saw it too, the small movement under her shirt, the tremor of life pressing against her stomach.

For a heartbeat, everything stopped.

Another kick, stronger this time.

And something inside her cracked open, something that wasn't fear.

Amelia's eyes flooded with tears. A sob escaped, softer this time. "She's moving."

Lucas nodded, his voice rough with emotion. "Yeah. She's

reminding you she's here."

She pressed both hands over her bump, shaking. Her breathing began to slow, her body loosening each time Ivy kicked.

Lucas lowered himself until his forehead rested against hers, his breath trembling.

"That's right, baby. She's got you. Both of us do."

Amelia let out a weak laugh that broke into a sob. "She saved me."

He kissed her temple. "No. You saved her, you keep saving her every damn day."

And in that small, flickering moment, between the blood on her palms and the kicks beneath her skin, Amelia finally let herself breathe again.

The blood on her palms hard dried. Faint crescent moons where her nails had broken skin. She didn't even realize she'd sat down until Lucas crouched in front of her again.

"I'm sorry," Amelia whispered.

He froze for just a second. "Don't be."

"I panicked. I let it take over. I shouldn't have…" Her voice cracked, "I don't want to lose myself again."

Lucas reached for her hands, and turned them over in his. His touch was gentle, but she could see how tense he was.

"You're not losing yourself," he said, grabbing the first-aid kit from the side table. "You're grieving. You're scared and I'd be more worried if you weren't."

He cleaned the cuts quietly, wrapping a bandage around each palm.

"I hate that I scared you," she said again. "I hate that you have to see me like this."

"I'd rather see you falling apart than not see you at all."

Her breath hitched.

Lucas guided her to the couch, easing her down like he didn't trust her legs to hold her much longer. He grabbed the blanket she always used and wrapped it over her shoulders.

Then he say beside her, pulling her close. "Close your eyes," he whispered. "Just for a minute. I'll be right here."

And she did. Tired. Frayed. Still shaking, but not alone.

Thirty

Chapter 30

The house was too quiet.

Lucas sat with Amelia curled into him, her head resting on his chest, her breathing finally even. Ivy kicked hard against his hand earlier, like she was fighting to bring her mother back.

And it worked.

But the stillness now didn't feel peaceful.

It felt like a held breath.

The knock shattered it.

Lucas stiffened beneath her. One single knock.

Not a neigbour.

Not a friend.

Amelia jolted upright. "Did you hear that?"

"Yeah. Don't move."

Lucas grabbed the pistol tucked beneath the couch. Quietly. Smoothly. He was already moving before she could say anything else.

He checked the hallway window first. No shadow. Then the front door camera.

A man stood alone at the edge of the porch. Hands raised. Face half-shadowed under a hood.

Not one of theirs.

Lucas opened the door only wide enough to point the barrel through.

The man didn't flinch. "I have a message for her."

Lucas stepped out, gun aimed. "You're breathing because I don't shoot messengers."

The man didn't speak. Just held out a piece of paper, trembling now.

Lucas snatched it and read it. His jaw clenched.

"Go," he said. "If I see your face again, I won't ask questions."

The man ran.

Lucas slammed the door and bolted it shut.

Amelia had followed halfway down the hall, pale and tight-lipped.

"What is it?"

Lucas didn't answer at first. He was staring at the note like it might catch fire.

She reached for it, but he pulled it away.

"I'll tell you," he said, folding it once. "But not here."

He led her to the kitchen, where Mason and one of the others were already coming in from the back, eyes alert.

"We've got another hole in the perimeter," Mason said. "Far side. North fence. Someone's been cutting wires."

Lucas handed him the note.

Mason read it, and for once, even he went still.

"What does it say?" Amelia asked, voice shaking.

Lucas's eyes met hers.

Tell her I'm coming for both of them. For Amelia. For Ivy.

Amelia's chest tightened. "But…how would he know Ivy's name? We only decided that yesterday."

The silence that followed said everything.

Lucas turned, barking orders. "Check the cameras. Sweep the perimeter. No one leaves this house, and no one comes in without clearance."

Mason's expression hardened. "You think we've been bugged?"

"I think he's listening," Lucas said. "Right now."

They searched every inch of the main rooms, walls, light fittings, beneath the couches. Mason pulled out a small device and swept slowly, inch by inch.

It beeped faintly near the bookshelf.

Lucas was there in seconds, ripping down a picture frame. Behind it, a tiny black dot was pressed into the plaster, barely visible. A recording device. Blinking red.

Amelia's knees went weak.

Mason yanked it out and smashing it against the hardwood. "It's live."

"How long?" Lucas growled.

"Hard to say. But if he heard Ivy's name…"

Amelia backed away, heart hammering. "He was in here. He was in this house."

Lucas caught her before she could spiral, his hands gripping her arms.

"We're safe now. We're sweeping the rest of the house. We'll burn this place down it we have to."

"But Ivy…"

"He's not touching her," Lucas said. "Or you. I swear to God."

Mason was already shouting into his comms, ordering a full sweep, metal detectors, reinforcements.

Amelia turned to look at the shattered listening device, and wondered what else Ethan had heard.

Lucas's knuckles hit the wall before anyone could stop him.

Once. Twice. Plaster split. Blood blooming against his knuckles.

"Lucas!" Mason grabbed his arm, but Lucas ripped free, shoving a chair so hard it splintered against the counter. "He's been listening in my house, Mason. He's been watching her… watching *them!*"

Every breath came jagged. The rage wasn't clean, it was panic in disguise. Fear that had nowhere else to go.

Amelia stood frozen in the doorway, her arms wrapped around herself.

"He always finds me," she whispered. "No matter where I go, he finds me. Maybe I really am cursed."

Lucas turned, chest heaving. His face broke open at the sound of her voice. "Don't say that."

Her voice cracked, thin and trembling. "Sophia's dead because of me. Now he's coming for Ivy. For you. It's all my fault."

"Stop," Lucas said quieter now, like if he raised his voice, she'd shatter.

He took a step forward, hand out, but she flinched back. Not from fear of him, from herself.

"I can't keep doing this," she said. "I can't keep pretending we're safe."

Before he could answer, Mason's voice cut through the

tension. "Lucas."

He was holding something, small and black glinting in the light.

A listening device.

"Found it behind the headboard in your bedroom."

Amelia's stomach dropped, "In our room?"

Mason nodded grimly. "It's live, or it was. Could've been transmitting for weeks."

Lucas's entire body went still.

He took the bug from Mason's hand, stared at it, then smashed it into the wall.

Amelia's legs gave out. She hit the floor hard, shaking. Her hands pressed to her belly, desperate and protective.

"He heard everything," she whispered. "He heard me. He heard us."

Lucas was there in an instant, crouching in front of her, voice rough but steady. "He's not hearing anything else. I swear to you."

He reached out, cupping her face. "Look at me. You and Ivy are still here. That's what matters."

Her breath came in sharp, uneven bursts, her hands digging into the carpet.

"Then why doesn't it feel like we're alive?" she whispered. "It feels like he's already buried us."

Lucas's voice broke, softer now. "Because you're exhausted. You've been fighting since the day you met me. But you're not alone in this fight. Not ever again."

He gathered her up, shaking, and carried her to the couch.

Mason stood at the doorway, silent, as Lucas whispered into her hair.

"I'll tear this world apart before I let him take one more thing from us."

The house had gone quiet.

Not safe. Just quiet.

Lucas stood at the kitchen sink, knuckles raw and bloodied, the skin torn where his fist had split the wall. Water ran red down the drain. He didn't feel it, not the sting, not the cold, just the weight in his chest.

Mason had gone back out to finish sweeping the perimeter. The others were radio silent, checking for more devices, eyes scanning every shadow.

Amelia lay curled on the couch, a blanket pulled to her chin. Her eyes were open but unfocused.

She hadn't spoken much since they found the second bug.

Lucas finished wrapping his hand, the bandage tight enough to stop the bleeding, not tight enough to stop the shaking though. He crossed the room and crouched beside her again.

"You okay?" he asked softly.

Amelia didn't answer. Her gaze flickered to the dark window, her body still tense, like she was waiting for the glass to shatter.

Lucas sat down beside her, not touching yet. Just breathing with her.

"I need to make things feel normal again," he said eventually. "Even if it's just for a minute."

Amelia blinked slowly, then looked at his hand. "You're bleeding."

"Not anymore." He smiled, faint and worn. "Just needed to feel something that wasn't fear for a second."

She shifted toward him, eyes tired. "Do you think it'll ever stop? The fear?"

He didn't answer right away. Instead, he reached for her hand, wrapping it in his, carefully and gently.

"I don't know," he said. "But I think if it ever does....it'll be with you."

She let herself lean into him, their foreheads touching in the soft dark.

No kisses. No fire. Just breath. Just bruised love and the sound of the wind scraping against the windows.

"Ivy's still safe," he whispered. "You're still here. And I'm not going anywhere. That's what I know."

Amelia exhaled, a shaky breath caught between grief and something close to peace.

And outside, somewhere in the night, the storm waited.

Thirty-One

Chapter 31

It was late. The house was quiet again. Too quiet.

Lucas stood near the window, eyes scanning the treeline through the curtain's edge. Mason's voice hummed over the radio in his ear.

"All patrols checking in. Front gate's untouched. East side is clear. No movement for the last hour."

Lucas didn't relax. Not even a little.

Amelia was in the bedroom, curled on the bed, one hand resting over the swell of her belly. Ivy had been kicking earlier. Soft, steady flutters like she knew her mother needed reminding she wasn't alone.

Lucas had kissed Amelia's forehead, whispered he'd be right down that hall, that she needed to rest.

But he didn't rest. Couldn't. Not with *him* still out there.

Ethan wouldn't give up.

And Lucas knew, deep in the marrow of his bones, that

tonight was the night something would crack.

Then the world tilted.

A soft, deliberate knock came at the front door. Not frantic. Not rushed.

Confident.

Lucas's blood turned to ice. The silence that followed was louder than any explosion.

"Mason," Lucas said, voice low. "Did one of ours knock?"

"No one's near the front entrance," Mason's voice snapped through the radio. "We didn't see anyone approach."

Lucas didn't speak again. He was already moving. Gun in hand.

Then came the sound.

Glass shattering down the hall.

Not from outside. From Amelia's room.

"Amelia!" Lucas screamed.

Mason shouted orders in the radio, his voice getting lost behind the sudden chaos. Gunfire outside, shouting at the gate, footsteps thudding along the house's perimeter.

Lucas ran down the hallway.

A scream tore to meet him.

Amelia's voice. "No! Lucas…!"

He burst into the bedroom, too late.

Three of Ethan's men were already in the room. One held Amelia by the wrist, wrenching her away from the bed. Another aimed a gun straight at Lucas's chest.

The third held a cloth, probably laced with something.

Lucas fired without hesitation. One shot. Straight between the eyes.

The man dropped.

The second spun, firing back. Lucas ducked behind the door frame. His shoulder grazed. The pain irrelevant.

Amelia kicked the man dragging her, sobbing. "Get off me!"

Lucas lunged, but the remaining man caught her from behind, wrapped an arm around her throat and pressed the muzzle of a pistol to her temple.

"Move, and she dies."

Lucas stiffened, breath catching hard, like he'd been punched straight through the ribs.

The man backed toward the window.

Glass crunched beneath his boots. The frame had been smashed from the outside.

"Don't you fucking touch her!" Lucas roared.

The man holding Amelia grinned. "Too late. She belongs to the boss now."

Amelia's eyes locked with Lucas's as she was dragged out of the window. Wide, wild and breaking.

Her belly seized tight, a crushing band of fear, and Ivy kicked so violently it hurt. Amelia sobbed, palms pressed uselessly to her bump as the man hauled her backward. "I'm sorry Lucas…"

He fired again, but missed.

They were gone.

The gunshot didn't stop the getaway van already revving in the trees. Lucas sprinted through the house, and past Mason screaming in the entryway.

Too many men.

Lucas reached the front yard just in time to see the van tear off into the night. Taillights glowing like demon eyes.

Gone.

Amelia was gone.

He stood in the yard, gun shaking in his hand. Blood dripping down his arm, heart ripped out of his chest. The team behind him slowly stopped firing. Mason limped to his side, face pale.

"We were outnumbered," Mason said. "He bought double the men."

Lucas didn't speak.

He just stared at the road where she vanished.

Then, finally, he breathed her name.

"Amelia."

Behind him, Mason spoke into the radio, barking orders. Calling out to every man they had on the ground, in the air, anywhere. But it didn't matter.

She was gone.

Amelia.

His girl.

Their baby

"Ivy…" Lucas whispered. And then he dropped.

His knees hit the cold earth hard, sending a jolt through his bones, but he didn't care. He stayed there, head bowed, fists clenched so tight the skin split across his knuckles. Dirt soaked into his jeans, but he was barely breathing.

Mason approached slowly. Unsure.

"Lucas…"

"Don't." The word cracked from Lucas's throat. He raised his head, eyes burning, teeth clenched like he was holding the whole world back by force of will alone.

"They took her," his voice was hoarse. "They walked into our home. Past our men. Through me."

"This isn't your fault," Mason said, but even he didn't sound convinced.

Lucas's lip quivered. "I swore she'd be safe. I *promised* her!"

He slammed his fist into the dirt, again and again until his skin split wider, blood mixing with soil.

"I'm going to burn them to the ground," he snarled. "I'll tear this whole fucking city apart if I have to. I'll find her."

Mason nodded, jaw tight. "We'll get her back."

Lucas looked at the house. The window where she'd been taken.

He stood slowly, shoulders trembling. "No more waiting. No more defense. We go to war."

And in that moment, whatever part of Lucas had been clinging to peace, to patience to mercy….

Died.

Thirty-Two

Chapter 32

Amelia blinked.

The ceiling was grey. Cracked. A single bulb buzzed above, casting a pale, flickering light that made her eyes ache. She tried to move and froze.

Her wrists were unbound, but her body…every inch felt wrong. Heavy. Numb.

She was lying on a mattress, thin and stained. Shoved into the corner of the room like an afterthought. No sheets, no pillow. Just a rectangle of sadness.

Her stomach turned.

Ivy.

Her hands flew to her belly. Still round. Still warm. Still *hers.*

Then the panic hit.

She sat up too fast. Dizziness crashed into her like a wave, but she forced herself upright, scanning the room.

Four walls.

No windows.

A single metal door bolted shut.

And in the far corner, a small plastic bucket.

That was it.

No water, no food, no clock, and no idea where she was.

Just a locked room and the slow, creeping wave of fear.

Her breath caught in her throat. She stumbled to her feet and threw herself at the door.

Bang. Bang. Bang.

"Lucas!" she screamed, fists pounding until her knuckles burned. "Lucas!"

No answer.

The silence was worse than a threat. It meant *he* was waiting. Watching.

Her voice broke. "Please…"

She backed away from the door, her body shaking. Tears blurred her vision, but she wiped them away, refusing to fall apart.

She looked down at her belly, and whispered, "I'm here, baby. I'm still here."

She sank to the mattress, arms wrapped around her bump, like it was the only thing tethering her to this world.

Because maybe it was.

The door opened with a slow hiss, and the stale air shifted.

Amelia didn't look up right away. She already knew who it was, the scent of his cologne, the sound of his shoes on the concrete.

Ethan.

He leaned against the door frame for a moment, watching

her like she was something on display. "You're quieter than I remember," he said softly. "Motherhood must've humbled you."

Her skin crawled. She pressed a hand to her belly without meaning to.

Ethan smirked at the gesture. "Ah. There it is. Instinct. I always wondered if you'd make a good mother. Thought about it a lot when you were mine."

He stepped closer, crouching in front of her, voice dropping low. "I used to imagine you carrying my baby. Not his. Mine. Would've been poetic, don't you think? The girl who thought she could run, tied to me forever."

Amelia's stomach turned. "You're sick."

He chuckled. "No, I'm practical. You were supposed to make me rich. But instead, you ran, took your pretty little body and your obedience with you. Do you know how much money I lost because of you?"

His voice sharpened. "Do you know what men would've paid to break you in half? To see you cry. To hear you scream my name while they ruined you?"

Amelia shook her head hard, tears forming. "Stop.."

But he didn't. He leaned closer, lips brushing the shell of her ear.

"I built an empire on girls who learned how to beg properly. And you were supposed to be my crown jewel. My perfect investment."

Her pulse thudded in her throat.

He drew back, studying her like a collector appraising something that had lost a little shine but still held value.

"Lucky for you," he murmured. "You've found a new way to pay me back."

Her breath caught. "What?"

He smiled, slow, hollow and obscene.

"You'll give birth here," he said, gesturing to the filthy mattress. "Right on that slab.

No doctors. No drugs. Just me. You'll bring her into the world the way you came into mine, screaming. And then you'll go back to what you were always meant to be. Mine to sell. Mine to use."

Amelia's eyes filled with tears. She shook her head, whispering through clenched teeth. "I won't let you touch her."

Ethan straightened, taking something from his pocket. A small square of paper. He dropped it beside her.

Her ultrasound photo.

"Of course you will," he said. "You'll hand her to me yourself. You'll beg me to keep her alive."

He smiled, slow and satisfied. "Ivy. Such a sweet name. I like it."

The door shut behind him.

The lock clicked.

And the silence that followed was worse than his voice.

Amelia stared at the photo, hands trembling. Her whole body shook, not from fear this time, but from something harder, sharper. Rage.

She pressed the ultrasound to her chest and whispered to the life inside her:

"He doesn't get to win. Not this time."

Thirty-Three

Chapter 33

The warehouse was empty.

Again.

Lucas stood in the middle of the cold concrete floor, chest heaving, knuckles still raw from punching through the drywall in the last room. Blood slicked across his hand, dripping onto the floor. Mason stood near the loading dock door, gun still in his hand, his jaw tight.

"Nothing," he said. "They cleared out hours ago. If they were ever here."

Lucas didn't respond. Couldn't.

He could still smell the acidic burn of exhaust fumes and old sweat. Like the place had been lived in. Briefly. Like someone had waited here just long enough to know they were being hunted.

And then vanished.

Just like the last place.

Lucas turned and drove his fist into the nearest steel beam, a roar tearing from his throat. The sound echoing off the walls, raw and unrestrained. His body vibrating with rage.

He'd failed her.

Again.

"Two fucking times," he growled. "Two fucking safe houses and we still can't find her!"

Mason didn't flinch. "We're going to. We just need…"

"We don't need more *time*, Mason. We don't have it."

Lucas looked down at his shaking hands. The blood. The dirt under his nails. All of it meant nothing if she was still gone. If she was still with *him*.

He dragged a hand through his hair, sweat sticking it to his forehead. "He's always one step ahead. Like he knows where we'll go before we do."

Mason's eyes narrowed. "You think there's still a leak?"

Lucas didn't answer. Didn't need to. The silence said enough.

He turned, stalking back toward the SUV parked outside the roll-up door. The night air hit him like a slap.

They'd checked every known property. Every name Ethan used. Every rat-hole the bastard had ever laid claim to.

And still, Amelia was gone.

Still, Ivy was gone.

His throat clenched.

She was scared. Alone. In pain. And he wasn't there.

Lucas leaned against the vehicle, head bowed, jaw tight. Then his knees buckled, not from exhaustion, but from grief.

He dropped to the ground like a man praying, both fists pressed into the dirt. The breath tore of out him in one ragged exhale.

"I swear to God," he rasped, voice shaking. "I will burn this entire fucking world down to get her back."

Mason stood a few feet behind him. Silent. Still.

"You really mean that?" he asked.

Lucas didn't lift his head. Just nodded once. "I'll rip out every piece of this city until there's nothing left but ash and blood."

A beat of silence, then Mason's voice, quiet and steady. "Then let's start with his dealers. We shake the streets until someone bleeds the truth."

Lucas stood slowly. Wiped the blood from his knuckles with the edge of his shirt. His eyes were colder than a bullet.

"Tonight. We don't stop. Not until we find her."

* * *

They found the second warehouse just after midnight.

Lucas kicked the door in before the others even got out of the car. He didn't wait. He didn't ask questions. He tore through the dark, gun raised, flashlight dancing over rusted metal and broken pallets. The stink of mold and gasoline filled his lungs.

"Clear left!" Mason shouted behind him.

Lucas didn't answer. He didn't care if it was clear. Not until he had her.

They'd already stormed two of Ethan's safe houses. Both empty. This one had to give him something. A name. A whimper. A shadow in the corner that knew where his girls were.

Amelia.

Ivy.

He tasted her name in the back of his throat. He hadn't slept. Hadn't eaten. His knuckles were still split from the last guy he'd made scream. And he'd do it again, a hundred more times if that's what it took.

They hit the back office, locked.

Lucas didn't hesitate. He drove his boot into the wood until the frame cracked, splinters raining down like sharp snow. The light inside flickered.

And there he was.

A small-time dealer. Sweaty. High as hell.

Lucas didn't speak. He crossed the room in three strides and slammed the guy against the filing cabinet.

"Lucas…" Mason warned, but it was too late.

Lucas had his gun pressed to the man's temple.

"Where the fuck is he?" he growled.

"I..I..don't…shit man. I don't know who…"

Wrong answer.

Lucas punched him. Hard. The man's nose crunched, blood gushing instantly. He sagged, whimpering.

"Don't lie to me," Lucas hissed. "You move Ethan's product. Girls. Pills. I know your face. I've seen the ledgers. Where the fuck is he?"

I don't…" The man cried out as Lucas grabbed his hair and yanked his head back. "Okay!

Okay! I heard…just heard, he's moving girls again. Said he got a 'fresh catch'. Said she was pregnant. A pretty one. Called her 'his favourite little liar.'"

Lucas froze.

Amelia.

"Where?"

The dealer whimpered. "Down near the river. The old ice plant. They gutted it. Set up cages, fuck man. I just drop shit off. I don't go inside."

Lucas dragged him forward and slammed him face-first into the desk. "You're going inside tonight."

"I…I can't. He'll kill me!"

"I'll do worse."

Lucas grabbed a rusty wrench off the shelf and brought it down onto the man's hand, shattering two fingers. The man screamed, shaking.

"You think Ethan's a monster?" Lucas snarled, crouching low. "You don't know a fucking thing about monsters. I'm what men like you have nightmares about."

The guy was choking on his own spit, trembling. "Please…"

"You should've begged Amelia for mercy," Lucas growled. "But you let him take her. So now you get to bleed for it."

Behind him, Mason placed a hand on his shoulder.

"Luc," Mason said softly. "We need him alive, to find her."

Lucas didn't blink. "Then he better start talking."

The dealer stammered more details, an alley near the docks. Unmarked black van. Late-night pickups. Men with masks, buzzed hair, one with a scar under his eye.

Lucas memorized every word. Burned them into his brain.

When they left, Lucas slammed the door shut, blood splattered across his shirt, hands aching.

"Pier, now." he ordered.

Mason raised a brow. You going to calm down before we get there?"

"No." Lucas loaded his gun and looked up, jaw tight, "I'm going to kill every last fucking one of them."

The pier was dead quiet when they arrived.

Salt in the air. Fog rolled in thick across the water. Lucas's boots hit the wood with heavy purpose, each step echoing like a countdown to war.

Mason and two others followed close, guns drawn, eyes sharp.

Lucas didn't speak. He didn't breathe right. His chest was a steel trap, every breath caught in a vice of rage and fear. His pulse was a war drum.

A black van sat near the loading bay. Just like the dealer said.

Lucas walked straight up to it, and yanked the doors open. Empty.

Not just empty, clean. Too clean. Scrubbed. Wiped. Bleached of blood and screams and her.

He turned.

"Warehouse," he barked.

They breached the side door in under ten seconds. The building was hollowed out, once used for shipping fish. Now gutted. Stripped. Metal cages bolted to the floor, most of them open.

Lucas froze in the middle of the room.

His fists clenched.

There was a faint trace of perfume in the air. Her perfume. She'd been here.

He missed her. Again.

He punched the wall. Hard. Again and again. Mason didn't stop him this time.

"She was here," Lucas rasped, voice low and dangerous. "I can feel it."

"Then he's staying on the move," Mason said grimly. "He's

trying to keep her invisible."

Lucas stared at the cages. Imagined her in one. Pregnant. Alone. Terrified.

Something inside of him shattered.

He turned suddenly and kicked a folding chair across the room.

"I'm going to fucking kill him!" His voice was like steel. I swear to God, Mason. I'm going to cut out his spine and watch him choke on it."

"We will," Mason said quietly. "But not tonight."

Lucas's chest heaved. He looked around, seething. "There has to be something. A name. A phone. Anything."

That was when one of the guys shouted from the back room.

"Boss! We found something."

Lucas stormed through the corridor, slamming the door open.

It was a phone. A burner. Battery still warm.

Lucas snatched it.

One recent text.

ETHAN: I wonder if she'll fight, or just cry when she meets the rest of my collection. Either way, she'll learn who she belongs to.

Lucas's breath caught.

He read it again and again.

Then he looked up, eyes wild. "We're running out of time."

Mason met his stare. "You're not sleeping tonight, are you?"

Lucas slipped the phone into his pocket and walked toward the door.

"Not until I have her back."

Chapter 34

The ropes bit into her wrists but she didn't struggle this time.

What was the point?

The mattress beneath her was thin. The sheet she had been given smelled like bleach.

Her ankles were bound too. Spread just wide enough to humiliate. Just tight enough to stop her from running.

Footsteps.

She flinched.

The door opened and in walked Ethan, followed by a man in a lab coat, far too clean for this place.

Amelia's breath hitched.

Ethan smiled. "Morning, sweetheart. Brought someone to check on my investment."

"Go to hell," she spat.

He leaned over her, eyes hungry. "We're already there, baby. And you're the only thing worth owning in it."

The doctor didn't meet her gaze. Just opened a worn medical bag and pulled on gloves.

"She's due for a check," Ethan said lazily, taking a seat near the wall. "Had a little scare with cramps the other week."

"Please, untie me," Amelia whispered, her voice hoarse with desperation. "I can't…I can't do this, like this."

The doctor didn't respond, didn't even look at her. He simply approached the bed, his eyes focused on her midsection. Amelia's heart raced as he peeled back the blanket, exposing her legs and the swell of her pregnant belly. She flinched at the sudden exposure, the cool air hitting her skin like a shock.

Her fingers curled into fists, nails digging into her palms so hard she felt the skin split.

Blood welled up under her nails, but she didn't scream. She didn't sob. She just turned her face toward the wall, trying to become nothing, to disconnect from the reality of her situation.

Amelia's breath hitched as she felt the cold metal of the speculum press against her, the instrument spreading her open despite her bound position. She bit her lip, as the doctor continued his examination, his gloves slick with lubricant.

Every movement was precise, almost mechanical, devoid of any humanity or compassion.

"Relax," the doctor said, his voice flat. "This will only take a moment."

Amelia wanted to scream, to kick, to fight, but she was helpless. Tears stung her eyes, but she refused to let them fall, refusing to give Ethan or the doctor the satisfaction of seeing her break.

The examination seemed to last an eternity. Finally, with a

soft click, the speculum was removed, and the doctor stepped back, his expression unreadable.

"She's stable," he said, his voice directed at Ethan, who stood in the corner, watching with a smirk. "Good growth, no signs of active cramping. Cervix is closed. But she needs rest. Too much stress could induce labor."

Ethan nodded, his eyes never leaving Amelia. "See that she gets it. I want that baby born healthy and strong."

The doctor nodded, beginning to pack up his tools. "I'll leave some medication to help with the cramps, if she needs it."

With that, they were gone. She lay there, staring at the wall, her mind a whirl of fear and despair. The baby kicked, a gentle flutter against her belly, a reminder of the life growing inside of her, a life she would do anything to protect, even if it meant enduring this hell.

* * *

The door creaked open.

Amelia didn't look up. She knew the weight of that silence, the way it slithered across the floor before him. She stayed still, tied to the bed, wrists raw and aching. Her skin sticky with sweat and humiliation.

"Look at you," Ethan's voice cut through the quiet. "Still pretty."

Her stomach twisted.

He walked closer. Food. The smell hit her like a punch. Greasy eggs, toast, a banana bruised at the edges. It made her feel nauseous.

"Didn't want you fainting on me, not with my little investment growing inside of you."

He set the tray on the table. Then came the slow, unbuckling of the leather straps.

His fingers brushed her skin like he owned it. She flinched.

"Eat," he said. "Can't have you starving Ivy. That'd be bad for business."

Amelia's hands trembled as she pulled the tray closer. She didn't want to eat, but Ivy needed her to. So she forced the eggs past her throat, each bite like swallowing sawdust.

Ethan watched.

"All that time wasted playing house with that fucker Lucas. But now? Now you'll be whatever I make you. A mother. A product. A toy. Whatever I need."

She didn't answer. Her hand gripped the fork tighter.

He leaned in, voice low, breath hot against her temple.

"After you give birth, I'll decide what to do with you. Maybe you get to raise her. Maybe you don't. Maybe you get to hold her once before I take her from you and remind you what losing feels like."

He pulled the tray away before she finished.

Locked the cuffs back around her wrists like she was a dog.

And left.

The door slammed shut with an echo.

Alone again.

The room felt colder.

But inside her, small and soft was warmth.

Tears ran silently into the pillow.

"It's okay, Ivy," she whispered. "You're strong, baby girl. Daddy's coming. He's going to find us. He's going to bring us home."

Thirty-Five

Chapter 35

~ ❧ ~

Mason's SUV tore through the winding roads, the engine growling with each turn. Lucas sat in the passenger seat, his body rigid with tension, his eyes fixed on the dark landscape flying by.

Two days. Two fucking days since Amelia had been taken, and they were no closer to finding her. The thought gnawed at him, a relentless, consuming rage that threatened to boil over at any moment.

"Lucas," Mason said. "You need to rest. You can't keep going like this."

Lucas didn't respond, didn't even acknowledge Mason's words. His mind was a whirlwind of images. Amelia's smile, her laughter, the curve of her belly where their child grew. The memories were both a comfort and a torment, a reminder of what he stood to lose.

Mason glanced at him, concern etched on his face. "You

haven't slept or eaten in days. You're not good to your girls like this."

Lucas's hands clenched into fists, his knuckles turning white. "I can't rest, Mason. Not until I have them back. Not until I know they are safe."

Mason sighed, his grip tightening on the steering wheel. "I know, man. I know. But you need to take care of yourself. For Amelia. For the baby."

The mention of the baby sent a fresh wave of anger and fear crashing through Lucas. He thought of Amelia, alone and terrified, and the baby, so vulnerable and innocent. His vision blurred, and he blinked rapidly, trying to clear the haze of exhaustion and emotion.

Suddenly, Lucas's control snapped. He slammed his fist into the dashboard, the impact sending a jolt of pain up his arm. "Fuck! Why can't we find her? Why can't we do something?"

Mason flinched, but kept his eyes on the road. "We're doing everything we can, Lucas. Every resource, every contact. We'll find her."

Lucas's breath came in ragged gasps, his chest heaving with the effort of holding back the storm of emotions threatening to consume him. "It's not enough, Mason. It's not fucking enough."

With a final, desperate cry, Lucas's body gave out. He slumped in the seat, his head falling back against the headrest, eyes closed. Tears leaked from the corners of his eyes, tracing paths down his cheeks. He felt Mason's hand on his shoulder, a steady grounding presence in the chaos.

"Let it out, man." Mason said softly. "You need this. You need to feel it."

Lucas let the grief and rage pour out of him, each sob a

release of the tension and fear that had been building for days. He thought of Amelia, of the life they had planned, of the future they had dreamed of. And he knew, with a certainty that cut through the fog of his exhaustion, that he would move heaven and earth to get her back.

As the SUV pulled up to the house, Lucas took a deep, shuddering breath. He had to be strong, had to be ready for whatever lay ahead.

Mason turned to Lucas. "You need to sleep. There's nothing more we can do tonight. You're running on empty and you can't help Amelia if you're not at your best."

Lucas's jaw clenched, and he shook his head, his eyes wild with a mix of exhaustion and desperation. "I can't sleep, Mason. Not until I know she's safe. Not until I have her back."

Mason reached out, placing a firm hand on Lucas's shoulder. "I get it, man. I do. But you're no good to her like this. You need to rest, to eat, to regroup. Tomorrow, we'll hit the ground running again, but tonight, you need to take care of yourself."

Lucas's body trembled with the effort of holding back the overwhelming tide of emotion and fatigue. He knew Mason was right, but the thought of resting, of doing nothing while Amelia was out there, was almost unbearable.

Mason gave his shoulder a squeeze, his voice gentle but firm. "Come on, Lucas. Let's get you inside. I'll make you something to eat, and then you can crash in your bed. You'll feel better in the morning. I promise."

With a heavy sigh, Lucas nodded. He followed Mason into the house, his steps slow and labored, each one an effort.

The house was quiet, too quiet, the absence of Amelia's

presence a palpable void that seemed to suck the life out of the room.

Mason led him to the kitchen, where he set about preparing a simple meal, sandwiches with a glass of water. Lucas watched him, his mind a blur of thoughts and images, each one more tormenting than the last.

"Eat." Mason, pushing the plate towards him. "And then get some sleep. I'll be right here, if you need anything."

Lucas nodded, his movements mechanical as he forced himself to eat, each bite a chore.

The food tasted like ash in his mouth, but he knew he needed the energy, needed to keep going for Amelia.

As he finished, Mason guided him to the bedroom, the room that still held the faint scent of Amelia's perfume. Lucas collapsed onto the bed, his body sinking into the mattress with a sigh of relief. He closed his eyes, but sleep eluded him. His mind racing with the thoughts of Amelia, of the baby, of the unknown.

Mason stood in the doorway, his voice soft. "Get some rest, Lucas. We'll find her. I promise."

With those words, Mason left, closing the door behind him with a soft click. Lucas lay there, staring at the ceiling, his body aching with exhaustion and his heart heavy with worry. He knew he should sleep, should rest, but the thought of closing his eyes, of surrendering to the darkness, was almost more than he could bear.

But as the minutes ticked by, his body finally gave in, pulling him down into a fitful, restless sleep, where dreams and nightmares blurred into one, a reflection of the chaos and fear that consumed him.

Thirty-Six

Chapter 36

Time no longer moved in hours.

It moved in kicks.

Amelia's hand trembled over the curve of her belly, her fingers tracing the skin like she was memorizing a map to a life she hadn't yet held. Ivy rolled beneath her palm, slow, sleepy movements, and it was the only thing that felt real anymore.

Not the cracked ceiling above her.

Not the worn mattress pressed to her spine.

Only Ivy.

The room was dim, the single light bulb overhead flickering like it couldn't decide if it wanted to live or die. The air was dry, heavy with silence.

The door creaked open.

Her whole body went still.

Ethan's shadow stretched across the floor before he entered.

"Good morning, sunshine," he said, like this was a dream and not a nightmare carved out of hell. "You're glowing."

Amelia didn't speak. Her jaw was locked tight, her arm protectively over her stomach. Ethan walked closer, something tucked under his arm. A folded piece of paper, thick and crinkled at the edges.

"I bought you something," he said casually. "Figured you'd want to see how the outside world's doing without you."
He dropped the paper on the floor at the foot of her bed, a tabloid. Her photo on the front.

"Missing and presumed dead," he murmured, crouching near her again. "Poor little Amelia. So tragic. And all the while, you're right here. With me. Growing more perfectly by the day."

Ivy kicked again, harder this time.

Amelia winced, curling around her belly. Ethan's eyes darkened with fascination.

"She knows me," he whispered. "She feels the truth in her blood. Just like you will. You were made for this. For me."

His fingers reached for her hair, she flinched before he even touched her. He laughed like she'd given him a gift.

"You'll give birth soon," he said, standing. "Then we'll decide what to do with you next. But don't worry, you'll always belong to me. You and Ivy. Forever."

He turned and left without another word.

The door slammed shut.

The lock clicked.

And she was alone again.

Amelia curled into herself slowly, her arms around her belly like a shield, like a prayer. She rocked gently, whispering to the life inside her.

"I'm here," she breathed. "I'm not giving up. Daddy's coming. He'll find us."

Her voice cracked, but she didn't stop.

"We just have to hold on."

The pain started low.

A dull, gnawing ache that throbbed just beneath her belly, tight and sharp like something was being pulled too far inside her.

Amelia sat upright on the thin mattress, her breath catching.

Not again. Please, not again.

Her hands cradled her stomach, trying to soothe the little girl beneath her skin. Ivy shifted, a gentle kick pressing against her ribs, still moving. Still here. Still okay.

But the pain didn't stop.

It tightened.

Cramped.

Sharp enough to make her curl forward, teeth sinking into her lower lip, to stop the scream threatening to break her open.

A sob slipped out anyway.

The door burst open.

Ethan's boots hit the floor like thunder, eyes dark and sharp as a blade.

"What did you do?" he snapped, storming toward her. "What the fuck did you do?"

Amelia shook her head, her lips trembling. "I…It hurts…my stomach."

"Fuck." Ethan spun around, already pulling out his phone. "She better not fucking lose it. I didn't keep you alive this long just to watch you fall apart."

Within minutes, the doctor was back.

Another man with cold eyes and rough hands. He didn't speak to her. Didn't offer comfort. Just nodded at Ethan and approached the bed, snapping on gloves like she was a body to examine, not a woman trying to survive.

"Don't touch me," she whispered, but her voice broke.

"You'll lie back and let him check," Ethan said with a twisted calm. "Or I'll let him do it with a knife."

Amelia froze.

The doctor checked her belly, pressed down hard enough to make her wince. Listened to Ivy's heartbeat with a stethoscope that smelled of rubbing alcohol and dust.

"She's still carrying," the doctor muttered. "The cramping's likely stress-induced. No signs of labor. Cervix is closed. Baby's heartbeat is strong."

Ethan exhaled like it was *his* child being saved.

"She needs to stay hydrated. Less panic, more rest. Or she'll go into early labor for real."

Ethan nodded once. "Then sedate her if you have to."

Amelia flinched. "No, please, don't drug me…please…"

But the doctor only left. No meds. Not yet. Just orders scribbled down for Ethan.

Once the door shut behind him, Ethan turned, and his face changed. Smoothed out like he was putting on a new mask.

"See?" he said gently, crouching beside her. "That wasn't so bad. You're still here. She's still here. All you have to do is *be good*. Stop stressing. Stop fighting. Accept what this is."

He reached out and cupped her cheek.

She didn't move. Didn't blink. Didn't breathe.

He smiled. "You'll be beautiful when you give birth. Radiant. Ripped apart just for me."

Then he stood and left, locking the door behind him.

Amelia curled into herself, her body still throbbing with cramps and fear. She whispered to her belly again, voice cracking as tears spilled.

"Ivy... I'm so sorry. I'm trying to keep you safe. I'm trying..."

She rocked gently, back and forth, like the motion might calm the storm inside her.

Like it might keep them both alive.

Thirty-Seven

Chapter 37

The walls bled silence.

Three months. Ninety-four days.

Lucas hadn't slept in more than two hours at a time since the night she was taken.

He sat at the edge of the long dining table in their house. Empty now but for the gun parts scattered before him like a puzzle he couldn't solve. A half-finished coffee had gone cold hours ago. The same as yesterday. And the day before that.

He hadn't eaten today. Or yesterday. Mason tried to keep count. Lucas didn't.

His ribs ached from grief. His jaw stayed clenched until it hurt to talk. His hands, scarred and cracked never stopped moving. If they stopped, he thought too much. If he thought too much, he saw her. Tied. Bleeding. Gone.

Mason entered quietly, a stack of intel folders in his arms, but Lucas didn't look up.

"Nothing from the ports," Mason said gently. "We hit the last known safe house on the east docks. Empty. Just like the others. No sign of her, no sign of him."

Lucas twisted the barrel of a glock in his hand.

"I'm missing something," he said hoarsely. "I'm fucking missing something."

"You're not."

"Yes, I am!" Lucas slammed the gun against the table. "I trained her. I trained all of you. We were ready for this. *How the fuck did he get her past us?* How did he just disappear with the mother of my child?"

Mason said nothing.

Lucas stood abruptly, pushing the chair back with a screech. He moved to the window, leaning one forearm against the glass as the cold seeped into his skin. He stared out at the pale morning sky, grey and sharp like a blade.

"She was wearing one of my shirts," Lucas said, voice low. "That morning. She made coffee. I kissed her temple."

He swallowed hard.

"She laughed when I told her she waddled."

Mason's voice was barely audible. "She's still alive."

Lucas turned sharply. "You don't know that."

"I do. Because if she wasn't, you'd be dead too. You'd feel it."

Lucas clenched his fists, fingernails slicing open old cuts. "I already do."

A knock at the front door shattered the silence.

Lucas moved like a loaded weapon, gun drawn, footsteps measured. One of his crew opened the door and handed over a plain, cream-colored envelope with no return address. Just one word scrawled across it in looping black ink:

LUCAS.

His stomach twisted. Mason stepped closer, eyes narrowing.

Lucas tore it open with trembling hands.

A photograph slipped free.

Time stopped.

Amelia.

Six months pregnant now, belly full and rounded under a threadbare dress. Her wrists were bruised. Her face was thinner. But her hand, her hand was resting gently over her bump.

A second page followed.

A note. Typed, not handwritten. Formal. Mocking.

You did good work, Lucas. Look how full she is.
I wonder who she'll beg for when the contractions start.
You? Or me?

Lucas didn't breathe. His fingers curled slowly around the page, then crushed it violently.

"Mason. Get. Everyone."

"Lucas..."

"NOW!"

The table flew against the wall, plates shattering like bones, coffee splashing down the wall. One of the legs cracked. A chair tipped and clattered to the floor.

Lucas dropped to his knees in the wreckage.

He grabbed the photo, careful not to touch the bruises on her skin. He touched her face with two fingers, his breathing ragged.

She was alive.

His baby was alive.

And he wasn't there.

"I swear to God," he whispered, voice shaking with hate, "I'm going to rip him apart piece by piece. I'm going to paint the walls with his blood."

He pressed the photo to his chest, forehead dropping to the floor. His voice cracked on the words:

"Hold on, baby. Please hold on. I'm coming."

* * *

The glass doors of CrossTech HQ slid open with a quiet hiss.

Lucas walked in like a storm barely held together by bone and breath.

The silence that followed him wasn't respect. It was fear.

Suits paused mid-conversation. Assistants froze with coffee cups in hand. Everyone had seen the articles. Everyone had whispered about *the woman* in the headlines. About *his girlfriend.*

About the baby.

One of the receptionists stood. "Mr. Cross... we're all so..."

He didn't stop.

Didn't blink.

Didn't look at her.

He just walked straight to the elevator, his hands clenched like he was holding himself together by force. The doors closed behind him, cutting the office floor off like a guillotine.

When they opened again, it was his top floor. His domain.

And even here, where he was king, no one dared speak.

He pushed through his private glass office doors and crossed to the hidden panel behind the bookshelf. One press of his palm and the biometric scanner beeped. A drawer slid out with a soft mechanical click, revealing an encrypted hard drive. His private server link, untouched by the public systems.

Lucas connected it to his workstation and sat.

The monitors flared to life.

Lines of code scrolled. Firewalls cracked. He bypassed every safeguard, every gate, diving into off-grid satellite data, military-level drone feeds, and digital breadcrumbs buried so deep only a man like him could pull them to the surface.

He didn't breathe.

Didn't blink.

Just hunted.

Behind him, footsteps.

Mara, one of his senior analysts, stood in the doorway, her voice gentle. "Lucas… we're all so sorry about…"

"Don't say her name." His voice was razor sharp.

Mara froze.

"She's not dead." He tapped a key, a photo pulled up. Blurred. Grainy. But there. Amelia. Barefoot. Pregnant. A timestamp from three days ago. A warehouse in a dead zone.

"I get these," he growled, "and nothing else. No trail. No trace."

Mara's mouth parted. "He's taunting you."

"No," Lucas muttered, eyes dark. "He's buying time."

He stood, fists clenching so tight the knuckles cracked. "He thinks I'll break. That I'll crawl."

He looked at her fully now, eyes like a grave.

"I'm going to rip this world apart until I find her."

Mara didn't speak. She just nodded. Quiet. Scared.

Lucas turned back to the monitors.

War was coming.

Thirty-Eight

Chapter 38

The air in the room was stale, thick with damp and rot. The mattress sagged beneath her, stained with time and tears, and the only light came from the thin strip beneath the bolted door.

Her back ached constantly now. Her feet swelled. She was six months along, and Ivy moved often, sometimes kicking so hard it knocked the breath from her lungs. But she welcomed it.

Ivy reminded her she was still alive.

Still fighting.

The lock clicked.

Amelia froze, hand splayed across her belly as the door creaked open and Ethan stepped inside.

He wore a smile that never reached his eyes. It never had. He held a metal tray, something steaming faintly, soup again. Water. A single orange.

"You're getting bigger," he said, setting the tray down. "She must be growing fast in there."

Amelia said nothing.

Ethan dragged a chair from the wall and sat by the bed, leaning forward with elbows on knees, watching her like she was some science experiment gone beautifully right.

His voice slithered through the dark. "Sometimes I wonder if you'll scream louder giving birth than you did when I broke you."

Her throat tightened.

He smiled wider.

"You'll scream, you know. I've heard it before, the way women break apart bringing life into this world. But you'll do it here. Right here. And I'll be the first thing Ivy sees."

Amelia's heart stuttered. Her fingers tightened protectively over her stomach.

Ethan tilted his head.

"She's mine, too, you know. Not by blood," he said, eyes gleaming, "but by fate. She was made under my watch. And you'll raise her how I say. Or you won't raise her at all."

"You won't touch her," Amelia finally whispered, voice shaking. "You won't come near her."

Ethan stood abruptly, smile snapping off like a switch. The air grew razor-sharp.

"You think you have a say?" he hissed. "You lost the right to fight when you chose him."

He stepped closer, but didn't touch her.

"You'll give birth here," he said again, voice low. "Then we'll see what kind of mother you make. Or if you're better used for something else."

He turned for the door.

Amelia sat frozen, breath shallow, heart pounding against Ivy's rhythmic thumps.

At the door, Ethan paused and looked back over his shoulder.

"I hope she has your eyes. It'll make it easier to break her."

The door slammed shut.

And the lock turned.

The light above flickered again, casting ghost-shadows across the walls of the locked room. Amelia sat on the floor, her back pressed to the far corner, legs curled under her growing belly.

She cradled the curve with both hands now, not just out of love, but protection.

"I will do anything to protect you, Ivy," she whispered into the quiet. Her voice sounded strange in this place. Too soft. Too human. Like it didn't belong here.

"I don't care what I have to survive. I don't care what he does to me." Her voice cracked. "He won't touch you. I'll die before he ever lays a hand on you."

A tear slipped down her cheek and fell onto her shirt. Ivy kicked lightly beneath her skin, as if reminding her she was still there. Still listening. Still holding on.

Amelia smiled, broken. "You're strong, just like your father."

She closed her eyes, letting the image of Lucas fill her mind.

"He has this look, baby. Like the whole world burns behind his eyes. But when he looks at me... it's like I'm the only thing keeping him tethered." She let out a quiet, breathless laugh. "He'd kill for you. I know he would. And he's coming. I promise you, he's coming."

Her arms wrapped tighter around her stomach as if shielding Ivy from the evil pressing in on all sides.

"I used to think I was cursed, you know?" she whispered. "That nothing good stayed. That everything I touched turned to blood. But then I had you. And somehow, despite all this darkness… you're still growing. Still kicking. Still here."

She tilted her head back and looked up at the ceiling, tears streaking silently down her face.

"I just need to hold on a little longer. Just a little longer, and he'll find us. And then I'll never let anyone take you away again."

She leaned forward and pressed her lips softly to the swell of her belly.

"I love you, Ivy. And your daddy does too. We'll be a family again soon. I promise."

Thirty-Nine

Chapter 39

The hum of servers was the only sound in the darkened lab, the glow of multiple monitors washing Lucas's face in cold blue light. He hadn't blinked in too long. Hadn't slept in longer. But he didn't move, didn't breathe, didn't dare hope.

Ping.

The sound cracked through the silence like a shot.

One of the monitors flashed. A signal. Weak. Scrambled. But there.

Lucas lunged for the keyboard, hands flying across the keys, decoding the packet with a frantic urgency that made his chest feel like it might cave in.

"Come on. Come on…"

CrossTech GeoNode 14-A: Signal Match - Device: Omega-7 | Traced Route: Intermittent – Locked Origin: Active.

His jaw clenched.

"Got you," he whispered.

Then he was on his feet, already storming out of the lab. Staff tried to speak. Apologies, condolences, whispers of sympathy, but he ignored them all. He was already halfway down the hall, fire in his lungs.

This time, he had something. And this time, he wasn't stopping.

* * *

The door slammed open as Lucas entered, wind and fury behind his steps. Mason looked up from the table where a map of the city was spread out, red markers stabbed into corners like wounds.

"You look like you've seen a ghost," Mason muttered.

Lucas tossed his phone down. "CrossTech caught a blip. A signal from one of Ethan's old comms. Not enough to get an exact location, but it's active. Which means he's somewhere close."

Mason straightened. "Shit. Where?"

"Outskirts. Industrial zone, where Ethan used to run girls before he started trafficking them out of the country."

Mason cursed under his breath, grabbing his jacket. "We go in hard?"

Lucas shook his head. "No. Not yet."

"What do you mean no?"

"If we go in too fast and he catches wind of it, he'll vanish. Again. Or worse..." His voice cracked slightly. "...he'll hurt her."

The room went still.

Lucas turned toward the map, fingers trailing the lines of streets and abandoned buildings like he could feel her out there. Her heartbeat. Her fear.

"I want eyes on every building in a five-block radius. Drones, street cams, paid informants. I don't give a fuck what it costs."

Mason exhaled, then nodded. "We'll get her back, man."

Lucas didn't look away from the map. His hand hovered over one marked in red. An old textile mill Ethan had used years ago.

"She's still out there," he said, voice low. "And I swear to God, Mason, when I get my hands on him… he won't be able to beg."

Lucas froze as the feed flickered into view.

His vision tunneled.

The room was small. Bare. Grey. Concrete. A mattress on the floor, a metal tray beside it with untouched food. One bucket in the corner like some kind of animal pen.

And there, curled in on herself, her arms wrapped around her belly was Amelia.

She looked thinner. Pale. Her hair was longer, tangled. But her stomach, fuck. Her stomach was round. Swollen.

Pregnant. Still carrying their daughter.

His Ivy.

His throat closed around the sound that clawed its way up, half agony, half a war cry.

Mason stepped forward, blinking at the screen. "Holy shit…"

Lucas didn't hear him. Couldn't.

He stepped back from the desk like the air had been sucked out of the room.

Then he moved.

Violently.

The chair slammed into the wall.

He grabbed a lamp and hurled it across the room, glass shattered, sparks flew.

Lucas's voice broke. "He's kept her locked away. Touching her, hurting her. I'll never forgive myself for letting this happen." His fists slammed the desk. Once. Twice. The edge split his knuckles open, blood dripping as he panted like a man possessed.

"She's six months," he rasped, eyes locked on the screen. "Look at her belly, Mason. That's our daughter in there. Ivy. He's keeping them both like fucking trophies."

Mason moved cautiously closer. "We're gonna get her out."

Lucas's voice was ragged. "I should've burned him to the fucking ground the first time. I should've ripped his heart out. But I let him live. I LET HIM LIVE."

The screen showed Amelia shifting slightly. Her hand moved over the swell of her stomach. Her lips moved, whispering something only Ivy could hear.

Lucas dropped to his knees like the weight of it all shattered him.

His bloodied hand pressed to the screen. "I see you, baby… I see you. Daddy's coming. I swear on every breath I have left, I'll kill him for touching you. I'll kill every man guarding that door."

Silence stretched.

Until Mason knelt beside him, jaw clenched. "We make a plan. We do this right. And when the time comes…"

Lucas met his eyes, wild and broken. "I don't leave until she's in my arms. Until Ivy feels my heartbeat through her mother's skin."

Mason nodded.

And Lucas, bloody, shaking, still on his knees lifted his eyes to the screen again. "Hold on, baby. Just a little longer."

Forty

Chapter 40

The concrete echoed with the heavy thud of Ethan's boots as he paced the corridor just outside Amelia's cell.

She'd stopped screaming weeks ago. Stopped begging. But he knew her spirit hadn't broken yet. Not fully. There was still that fire in her eyes every time she looked at him, like she was just waiting to sink her teeth into his throat.

He loved that about her.

"She's real pretty with that belly now," he said to no one in particular, a grin twitching on his lips as he lit a cigarette. "Carrying my retirement plan in her ribs."

One of his men lingered awkwardly near the edge of the hallway. Small, wiry, nervous.

Ethan blew out smoke through his nose. "You got something to say, or are you just here to breathe my fucking air?"

The guy flinched. "Boss... we picked up some chatter. Nothing solid, just... noise."

Ethan tilted his head, smile gone. "What kind of noise?"

"Lucas. They say he's asking around again. Streets are tighter. Word is he hit two of our old stash spots."

Ethan stepped forward slowly, deliberate. The guard tried not to shrink back, but Ethan could smell fear like blood in the water.

"Lucas…" he repeated, almost wistfully. "Still clawing at the dark like a good little dog."

He grabbed the man by the jaw, fingers digging into flesh. "Let me tell you something. That little bitch? She's mine. My blood, my pain, my fucking profit. And her hero? He's gonna die screaming."

The man nodded as best he could in Ethan's grip. "Yes, sir."

Ethan shoved him back. "Double security on the lower tunnels. Check every fucking camera. If he so much as breathes near this place, I want to know before he does."

He flicked his cigarette to the ground, crushed it under his boot, and turned to face the door behind him.

Behind it, Amelia lay. Still stubborn. Still alive. Still carrying the baby he would take from her one way or another.

"She'll learn," he whispered to the steel. "They all do." The concrete echoed with the heavy thud of Ethan's boots as he paced the corridor just outside Amelia's cell.

She heard it through the vents first, muffled conversation in the corridor outside her locked door. Then clearer. Sharper.

"…Lucas is getting closer," a man's voice said.

Her blood turned to ice.

"Let him come," Ethan snapped, cruel amusement lacing every word. "He can dig up my old spots, bleed my rats dry, he'll never find this place. Not until I'm done."

There was a pause. A cigarette flicked, maybe. A footstep.

"I should send him another photo. Maybe one of her belly this time. Stretch marks and all. Think he'll cry? Think he'll kill for it?"

Laughter echoed. Then a harsh slam of a hand against something metal.

Amelia didn't realize she'd started shaking until her hand slipped from her stomach.

She curled into herself, breath catching in her throat.

She wanted to scream. To claw at the walls. To throw herself against the door and never stop pounding until the world cracked open.

But she didn't.

She swallowed her scream and laid her hand back across her belly.

"Ivy…" she whispered. "It's okay, baby. He doesn't get to win. Not this time."

She blinked against the stinging heat in her eyes.

"Daddy's coming for us. He loves us. So much. And I love you. I love you so much it hurts."

Ivy kicked, harder this time.

Amelia almost sobbed with relief.

She cradled her bump and whispered stories into the quiet. About Lucas. About safety. About the beach house she once saw in a dream where the waves sang lullabies and no monsters lived in the dark.

She was curled into the mattress when the door sighed open. Already braced, because everyone who came through that doorway came with teeth.

Ethan stepped into the room, his movements deliberate and

calculated, as if he had rehearsed this moment a thousand times. The tray in his hand clinked softly, the faint smell of boiled cabbage and bleach lingering in the air. He set it down on the rickety table with the careful precision of a man placing a prized possession on a shelf.

"Look at you," Ethan crooned, his voice a sickly sweet syrup that seemed to seep into every crack of her being. "All quiet. All soft for the little one."

Amelia didn't look up. Instead, she pressed her palm to her belly, fingers splayed as if she could shield the small life inside from the very air around her.

Ethan moved closer, his shadow falling across her like a dark curtain. He crouched at the edge of the bed, so close that she could smell the cheap cologne and the stale smoke that clung to him. His eyes, once familiar, now held a dangerous hunger, a pride that was both terrifying and revolting.

"You know," he said, voice casual as a blade slipping between ribs, "they plaster your face everywhere. Cry for you. Pray you'll come home." He tapped her stomach, each touch a warning. "But I keep what belongs to me."

His words slid under her skin, and Amelia's fingers tightened reflexively over the swell of her shirt, as if she could protect the life within from his twisted words.

Ethan's eyes gleamed with a dangerous light. "You should be grateful, Amelia. Most girls never get this kind of attention. A private room. Food. Company. A doctor who checks you over. You're in the top tier."

Amelia forced air into her lungs, her voice barely a whisper. "Don't. Don't you dare…"

He cut her off with a small, pleased laugh. "You still have teeth. Good. It makes this more entertaining."

His hand landed on the mattress beside her shoulder, the pressure of it pinning the edge of her body to the bed without actually touching her where she curled. Not quite gentle, not quite brutal. A reminder that he could control the room with the mere weight of his arm.

Ethan leaned in closer, his breath hot on her cheek. "Once you give birth," he whispered, his voice thick with anticipation, "and I taste this pussy again, it's going to make me so much money."

"Listen." He reached into his satchel and pulled out a battered stethoscope, the rubber tube coiled like a snake. He laid the cold metal on her belly and leaned in, as if he wanted to hear her fear as much as the baby's heart.

Amelia's breath thinned. Ivy's faint, steady thud thrummed like a promise beneath the metal.

Ethan closed his eyes and smiled the slow, sick smile of a man tasting victory. "Strong," he said softly. "Strong little thing."

She wanted to yank the stethoscope off, to shove the plastic away like it was a snake, but the motion felt useless, and he was watching, enjoying the hesitation.

"You think he'll come for you?" Ethan asked after a long beat, voice conversational, as if they were discussing the weather. "Your hero in his suit, smashing down doors, rescuing damsels. Cute image."

A cold ball of rage and dread rolled through Amelia. "He will!"

"You sound hopeful." He tapped the rim of the stethoscope, eyes hooded. "Hope is fragile. Hope is loud. I prefer the quiet. Quiet is easier to manage."

He lifted the metal from her belly and pressed his palm flat on the fabric.

"If he comes for you," Ethan said, voice low and loving as poison, "he'll have to decide: do I let him have his precious Amelia, or do I make him watch what happens to women who disappoint me?"

Amelia's hands clenched. Ivy kicked, sharp and insistent, like an answer. Ethan watched the motion with an unreadable expression, then straightened as if bored by the display.

"Eat," he ordered suddenly, nodding toward the tray. "You need to keep the little one fed. You wouldn't want your daughter to be weak on my account."

She pushed food away. He slid the plate back into place with a patient, practiced gentleness. "Fine," he said. "If you won't eat for me, eat for her. I like when things go according to plan."

He stood at the threshold then, one shoulder pressed to the frame like a man lounging at a show. "Sleep well," he added, voice soft with mock-sympathy. "You'll need your strength for what's coming."

The door shut on the click of the lock. The sound fell like stone.

Alone, Amelia pressed her forehead to her stomach and mouthed the words she'd learned to keep herself from breaking.

"We'll get out. Daddy is coming. Hold on for him. Hold on for me. Hold on for Ivy."

Her hand trembled across the swell of the life inside her. Ivy nudged, answering an urgent, tiny push as if to say, *I am here. I am still here.*

Outside, in the corridor, Ethan's laugh drifted for a heartbeat and then it was gone. A sound that would haunt her sleep.

Chapter 41

The door opened. She heard it before she saw him. The heavy tread of boots, the lazy sigh of metal against frame. Not Ethan. One of his men. The younger one. Nervous.

Amelia didn't hesitate.

The moment he stepped inside, she moved.

She'd spent weeks counting steps from the bed to the door. Weeks memorizing every creak in the floorboards and mapping the weak spots in her guard's attention.

She grabbed the rusted edge of the food tray with both hands and slammed it into the guard's face with everything she had. The clang rang out like a gunshot. He staggered back, cursing, blood already rushing from his nose.

She didn't wait.

She launched herself past him, heart thundering, the sudden movement wrenching her stomach. Pain lit up her side. Ivy kicked, a terrified lurch that made Amelia's own breath vanish in a gasp.

Not now. Please not now.

She ran.

The hallway was longer than she remembered. Colder. Shadows twisted against the bare light bulbs overhead. Her feet hit the floor in rapid slaps.

The door at the end… *maybe it led outside, maybe…*

A body slammed into her from the side.

She screamed, not in fear, but rage. Pure, primal, helpless rage as another man, thicker, stronger caught her mid-sprint and dragged her back. Her fists flailed. She bit down hard on his arm, tasted blood and sweat and filth.

"LET GO OF ME!"

He shoved her. Too hard. Her knees hit the floor. Her stomach jarred.

Pain shot through her. Low, deep, spreading like fire across her abdomen.

"No, no, no…." She curled around herself, one hand on the wall, the other over her belly. Ivy shifted, slow and sluggish. Still moving. Still there. But everything in her screamed wrong.

And then he was there.

Ethan.

He stepped into the hallway like he'd just walked into church. Calm, pressed shirt, sleeves rolled, and fury etched into every line of his face.

The man holding her backed away immediately.

Ethan looked at her like she wasn't human.

"You," he said coldly, "were told to rest."

She didn't speak. Couldn't. Her body was too busy shaking. Her vision swam. Her shoulder ached from where she'd hit the floor, but none of it mattered. Only Ivy. Only the baby.

"You could have lost her," Ethan said. His voice was quiet, but it dripped venom. "You risked *my* child."

Amelia lifted her chin. "She's *mine.*"

His eyes darkened. "She's *ours,*" he corrected, then knelt in front of her. "And I will not let you destroy what I've built because you had a tantrum."

She tried to slap him.

He caught her wrist mid-air, twisted it gently, just enough to make her wince.

"No more games," he said.

Then he stood, nodded to the guards. "Take her back. Gently."

They did. She didn't fight them this time. Her body was already screaming, her heart fracturing under the weight of her own failure.

Amelia lay still for a long time, staring at the ceiling. Her hands trembled as she smoothed her shirt down over her stomach, her mind replaying the words *strong heartbeat* over and over like a prayer.

But her chest still ached. Her ribs still hurt from where she'd hit the floor.

And deep inside, low and sharp something twisted.

A cramp.

At first, she told herself it was nothing. Just tension. Just fear. But then another came, tighter, like a hand closing inside her.

She gasped. Her hands flew to her stomach. "No… no, please, not now."

She rolled onto her side, curling protectively over the bump, her breathing quick and shallow. Her body shook as the pain spread through her hips, her thighs.

And then she felt it.

Warm.

Wet.

Her hand came away red.

Panic clawed its way up her throat. "No," she whispered, her voice breaking. "Please, Ivy… stay with me, baby, please…"

Her cries echoed against the walls. She tried to sit up, but her legs gave out under her. Her body was too heavy, too weak.

She reached for the door, pounding it with her fist. "Help! Please, someone!"

It took seconds that felt like years before the lock clanked open.

The same guard who'd dragged her back earlier froze in the doorway at the sight of the blood on her hands. He yelled something down the hall, a barked order and then Ethan appeared, all composure gone.

For the first time, she saw fear on his face.

"What did you do?" he demanded, crossing the room in two strides.

"Please," she sobbed. "It's not me…it just started…"

He turned on the guard, his voice a snarl. "Get the doctor. *Now.*"

The doctor stumbled back in, half-awake, pulling gloves on with shaking hands. "Move," he told Ethan. "I need space."

Ethan backed away, pacing, hands in his hair. "If she loses that child, I'll…"

"Out," the doctor snapped.

He obeyed.

The exam was quick, clinical, brutal. The doctor's breath came fast through his nose. Amelia couldn't stop shaking.

After what felt like forever, he looked up. "You've got a partial placental abruption. A small part of the placenta has torn away from the uterine wall. Likely from the trauma. Your stable for now, but if you move, if you so much as try to stand, it could get worse fast. That means absolute bed rest. No stress. No sudden movement. Hydration and monitoring. If it gets worse, you'll bleed out before anyone can help."

He glanced at Ethan, jaw clenched. "If you want her alive, you'll keep her calm. Any more stunts, and you risk losing both mother and baby."

Amelia's hands shook as she pulled the blanket around her, pain still echoing through her core.

Amelia broke down. Sobbing so hard her body curled around itself.

The doctor squeezed her wrist lightly, the only human gesture he'd ever shown her. "You're lucky," he said softly. "So is she."

Then he left.

Ethan reappeared a moment later, standing in the doorway, breathing hard. His eyes roamed the blood smeared on the sheets and the trembling woman in front of him. Something inside him snapped quiet.

"You ever scare me like that again," he said, his voice terrifyingly calm, "and I'll chain you to the bed until that baby's born."

He shut the door gently, like he didn't trust what would happen if it slammed.

Amelia lay there, soaked in sweat and tears, her hand pressed flat over her belly.

"I'm sorry," she whispered. "I'm so sorry, Ivy. I'll be better. I promise."

Then, faint, a flutter.

A kick.

Alive.

She broke on a sob, whispering again and again, "We're still here."

Chapter 42

The SUV skidded to a stop in a cloud of dust and fury. Lucas was out before the engine fully cut, gun in hand, eyes scanning the perimeter of the rundown farmhouse CrossTech had finally triangulated.

Mason was right behind him, weapon raised. "Signal came from here," he confirmed, jaw tight. "Popped up an hour ago. Long enough for a trace."

Lucas didn't waste time. He kicked the door in, the wood splintering under the force.

"AMELIA!" he roared.

The house was empty. Cold.

A half-eaten plate of food on the kitchen bench. A chair knocked over.

Lucas stormed through every room like a man possessed. "AMELIA!" he yelled again, shoving open the basement door and descending two steps at a time. But the space was vacant, just a single mattress and a bloody cloth on the floor.

He stared.

His fists clenched. "She was here," he whispered. "She was just fucking here!"

He ran a hand down his face, breath catching.

Mason stepped into the doorway. "We missed them. Maybe by an hour. Maybe less."

Lucas turned slowly, his voice hollow. "He knew."

Mason nodded. "He's moving her. He knows we're close."

Lucas's eyes locked on the mattress again, the only sign of her. He walked over and knelt, fingers brushing the sheet. His face twisted.

"She bled here," he said. "She was hurt."

He slammed his fist into the cement floor with a guttural yell. "*I was so fucking close!*"

Mason didn't speak. There was nothing he could say.

Lucas sat there, chest heaving, eyes burning, staring at the remnants of his girl's suffering.

Then: a whisper of fabric.

He turned.

Something small was tucked behind the pipe. A button. Pale pink.

He picked it up, one of the buttons from a shirt.

His throat closed.

"She left this for me," he murmured. "She knew I'd come."

Mason's voice was quiet. "We'll find them. You have my word."

Lucas stood, button clutched in his hand like a talisman. "I'm not stopping," he growled. "I don't care if I have to tear down every building, pay off every rat, or put a bullet in every man Ethan's ever touched."

He looked up, fire behind his eyes.
"He took my girls. Now I'll take everything from him."

Forty-Three

Chapter 43

The van smelled like sweat, metal, and gasoline. Her wrists ached from the zip ties, rough plastic biting into skin rubbed raw by weeks of captivity. One of Ethan's men sat across from her, armed, unsmiling. The other beside her kept a firm grip on her shoulder, like she might vanish if he let go.

She wouldn't.

She couldn't even *run* anymore. Not with the way her body ached. Not with the way Ivy stretched and shifted inside her, growing heavier by the day.

The road beneath them jolted. Her back throbbed. A sharp pull beneath her ribs made her wince.

"She okay?" the man beside her asked the other.

"She'll be fine," the one across from her said flatly. "He said to get her there *alive*. That's it."

Amelia didn't speak. She kept her head low, heart hammering, but her mind raced.

They were moving her again. *Why now?*

Was Ethan scared? Was Lucas getting close?

God, she hoped so.

They slowed. Turned. Gravel crackled under the tires. A gate opened.

She peeked through the tiny slits in the rear door.

Not a city street.

Woods.

Isolated.

Her throat tightened.

When the van came to a stop, the doors opened, and cold air slammed into her lungs.

"Out."

The guard grabbed her arm again and pulled her to her feet.

As they turned to unlock the new door, Amelia reached beneath the edge of her shirt. With shaking fingers, she yanked it over her head. She said her stomach was cramping. She said she needed to breathe. The guard grunted and let her sit on the step while he went ahead to clear the hallway.

She balled the shirt in her lap and *wedged it deep* into the hollow beneath the back stairs, beside an overgrown bush. Not visible to the guards. But maybe… maybe Lucas would see it.

Maybe he'd *feel* it.

Just like he used to feel her heart before she ever spoke a word.

"Please," she whispered into the dark. "Find me. Find us."

The next moment, rough hands grabbed her and hauled her inside.

This place was different.

Colder.

Concrete floors. No windows. Just a long hallway lined with heavy doors, each with a sliding slot near the bottom. Like feeding slots.

Cells.

Her legs trembled.

They shoved her into one of the rooms. A mattress on the floor. A rusted bucket in the corner. A single flickering light overhead.

Then the door slammed shut.

No locks on the inside.

No voice to scream loud enough.

Just her.

And Ivy.

She cradled her belly and leaned against the wall, whispering through the rising tears.

"Your daddy's looking for us. I know he is. I left him a piece of us, baby girl. We just have to hold on."

The room had no windows.

No sound except for the buzz of the overhead light and the rhythm of her own breathing. Shallow, too fast, like her lungs had forgotten how to work properly in the dark.

Eight months.

The walls pressed in closer now. Her belly stretched taut beneath the faded shirt that barely fit. Her ankles swelled. Her back ached. Her mind….her mind was going.

She knew it.

It was in the way she talked to Ivy like she was already born. Like she could answer back.

It was in the way she touched the wall like it could open. Like it could *bleed* like her.

"Ivy," she whispered, rubbing her thumb in slow circles over the curve of her stomach. "You're so close now. Just a few more weeks, baby girl."

She hadn't seen the outside world in months.

She hadn't seen the stars.

The air here tasted like damp stone and mold. The floor was always cold, even when Ethan brought a heater. And the silence… it was worst at night, when she could *hear herself unraveling*.

Sometimes she forgot what Lucas looked like.

And then she'd panic, because how could she forget the man who taught her how to breathe again?

She'd cry herself hoarse whispering his name.

"Lucas is coming," she murmured now. "He's coming, Ivy. I don't know when, but he *will*."

Tears burned down her cheeks as she pressed her forehead to her knees.

"He has to."

Her hands shook. Her skin felt like it didn't belong to her anymore. Stretched thin over something hollow.

"I miss him so much," she said through a sob. "And I hate that you'll come into this world without him here to hold you."

She curled onto her side on the stiff mattress, one arm around her stomach, the other fisted in the fraying sheet.

"I'll do anything to keep you safe. Even if I have to die for it."

She flinched as the lock on the door clunked.

Heavy boots on the stairs.

Her muscles seized. Her breath stalled.

She could always tell the difference between the guards and *him*.

Ethan's presence moved like oil down her spine. Slick.

Heavy. Smothering.

But when the door opened… it wasn't him.

It was one of the younger ones. New.

He didn't say anything. Just set down a tray of food and backed out.

She watched the door close again. Listened to the bolt slide home.

And then she broke.

A jagged sob tore out of her chest, her body curling tighter around Ivy, like she could shield her from a world already soaked in violence.

The tray sat untouched.

She didn't even flinch when a mouse scurried past the corner.

All she could do was count her breaths. One for her. One for Ivy.

Over and over.

Until there was nothing left but silence again.

The lock clicked again.

This time, she didn't look up.

The air in the room shifted before he even stepped inside. That crawling, suffocating heaviness that always came with him. Like the oxygen itself turned poisonous when Ethan was near.

"Amelia," he said softly, like her name was something sacred. "You look tired, sweetheart."

She didn't answer. She couldn't.

Her throat was dry, her tongue heavy. The smell of him. Cologne and sweat and something metallic, filled the space and made her stomach twist.

He crouched down beside the bed, fingers brushing her hair from her face. "I told you this place would keep you safe."

"Safe?" Her voice cracked on the word. "You mean trapped."

He smiled, the kind that made her skin crawl. "Trapped, safe… same thing, isn't it? You're still breathing. The baby's still alive. That's all that matters."

Amelia flinched when he leaned closer, his lips grazing her temple, slow and deliberate.

It wasn't a kiss, it was ownership.

It made her stomach turn so violently she thought she might be sick.

"Please don't," she whispered. "Don't touch me."

"Still so dramatic," Ethan murmured, ignoring her plea. His hand slid down, fingers tracing the curve of her swollen belly. "Not long now until you give birth, my sweet. You've done so well keeping her safe for me."

"She's not *yours*," Amelia hissed through her teeth. "She'll never be yours."

Ethan's eyes lit up with something cold and gleaming. "You said the same thing about yourself once."

He tilted his head, studying her face like he was memorizing her fear. "I'm going to have the doctor check you over again. We can't have my little girl coming early, can we?"

"She's *mine*," Amelia said, the words breaking into a whisper. "She's mine and Lucas's."

Ethan's smile faltered for a second. Then it hardened. "Lucas doesn't even know if you're alive anymore. He's probably moved on. Found someone else to fill your place."

Her chest cracked open with pain. "You're wrong."

"Am I?" He leaned in, his mouth hovering at her ear. "You'll see soon enough. You'll give birth here, and then you'll learn what it means to belong again."

He pressed a kiss to her cheek, gentle, deliberate and she jerked away, trembling.

"Don't do this," she whispered, tears sliding hot down her face. "Please, Ethan. Don't…"

"Shh." He stood, smoothing his jacket like he hadn't just destroyed another piece of her. "Be good for the doctor. We wouldn't want anything to happen to Ivy now, would we?"

When he left, the sound of the lock sliding home was louder than the click of a gun.

Amelia crumpled forward, hands trembling as they pressed over her stomach.

"Ivy," she whispered, her voice shaking, "you stay strong, baby. You don't listen to him. Your daddy's coming for us. I know he is."

The door opened again an hour later.

Boots. The metallic scrape of a tray. The faint smell of antiseptic that made her stomach roll.

Ethan stood in the doorway with the doctor.

The same one as before. Pale, gaunt, eyes hollowed out by fear. He didn't look at her as he entered. No one ever did.

Ethan said flatly. "Make sure she's fine. I don't want anything happening to my investment."

Amelia's jaw locked at the word.

Investment.

She wanted to scream, but the sound caught in her throat when the doctor pulled on gloves.

"Lay back," he said quietly.

Her hands trembled as she obeyed, every muscle wound tight as he began his exam. The gloves were cold. The touch clinical. Detached. Still, the humiliation burned down to her bones.

"She's eight months," the doctor muttered, voice tight. "The baby's under stress. You said she's been having cramping?"

Ethan crossed his arms. "Sometimes. She complains a lot. You doctors always exaggerate."

The doctor shot him a look. "She's showing signs of strain. Her blood pressure's high. There's tenderness here."

Amelia flinched when his hand pressed against her belly. "You keep this up, and she could go into labor early."

Ethan's face darkened. "Then fix it."

The doctor swallowed hard. "I can't *fix* a pregnancy, Mr. Walker. She needs rest. Water. Proper food. She shouldn't even be here."

Amelia's vision blurred with tears. "Please," she whispered, "I just want to go home."

Ethan crouched beside her, his hand resting heavy on her stomach. His touch made her skin crawl.

"You *are* home," he said softly. "You'll give birth here, under my roof. You'll bring Ivy into my world, where she belongs."

"She'll never belong to you," Amelia hissed.

Ethan smiled, slow and cruel. "That's what you said before I took you back, too."

He stood abruptly. "Keep her breathing. Keep her quiet. I don't care how."

Then he was gone.

The door slammed. The lock turned.

The doctor hesitated. "He's getting worse," he whispered. "You need to stay calm, Amelia. Stress will trigger labor."

She swallowed hard, staring up at the flickering light. "She's okay?"

"For now," he said. "But if you keep bleeding like this…"

He didn't finish.

He didn't have to.

When he left, she curled on her side, hands over her stomach, whispering to the only thing in this place that still felt like hope.

"It's okay, Ivy," she breathed. "We just have to survive a little longer. Daddy's coming."

The words trembled like prayer.

Forty-Four

Chapter 44

The map was a blur of red pins, half-torn notes, and coffee stains. Weeks of nothing. Months of false leads. Every second felt like glass under his skin.

"She'd be close now," Lucas muttered to himself, voice hoarse. "Due any damn day."

He sat hunched over the CrossTech interface in the dim-lit room, hands shaking as he scrolled through new pings. Desperate for anything, anything that hadn't already turned to dust.

A cold sweat clung to the back of his neck. He hadn't slept. He couldn't. Not when Amelia was somewhere alone. Not when his daughter was growing inside her, full-term now.

Mason stepped into the room cautiously. "Boss…"

Lucas didn't look up. "Say you've got something."

Mason hesitated, then dropped a printed aerial image beside him. "We ran a new satellite scrape using CrossTech's deep thermal scans. One signal, off-grid, hitting every anomaly filter. Locked down tighter than any warehouse I've ever seen."

Lucas stared at it. A single dot on a sea of black.

"She's there," he said.

Mason ran a hand through his hair. "If we go in and it's nothing."

"I *don't* have another month, Mason." Lucas stood so fast the chair crashed behind him. "She's eight months. Eight. I missed the baby growing inside her. Missed every flutter, every kick. You think I'm missing the goddamn birth?"

Mason opened his mouth, but Lucas was already storming out.

"I swear to god," Lucas snarled, grabbing his gun, "if he's touched her, if he's laid one *fucking* hand on my girls. There won't be anything left but bones and blood."

He slammed his fist into the door frame on the way out. A splinter of wood cracked beneath the force.

No more delays. No more mercy.

Lucas wasn't a man anymore. He was war. And nothing would stop him this time.

Lucas stood over the new satellite prints Mason had just thrown down on the table. His jaw clenched so tight it ached, knuckles white as he gripped the edge of the bench.

"There," Mason said, stabbing the page. "That convoy? That's not local. Not scheduled. Private, unmarked. They moved her."

Lucas barely blinked. "How long ago?"

"Hour, maybe less. We're close. I swear it, man we're nearly there."

Lucas nodded once, slow and dangerous. The calm before a

storm. "Get the gear ready. We roll tonight."

Mason hesitated. "We need eyes first. Intel. If they're moving her, they'll be paranoid. Could be booby-trapped. Could be…"

"I *don't care*," Lucas snapped, turning, his voice low and lethal. "That's my family. My daughter. You think I give a shit about traps?"

Silence stretched for a beat before Mason gave a grim nod. "Alright. Let's do it smart but fast."

Jax shoved open the door, phone in hand. "Boss, CrossTech just pinged a hot signal. Security feed. Ethan's setup must've glitched or shifted just enough to expose a network. We've got a visual."

Lucas spun, grabbing the tablet.

There she was.

Amelia.

On screen, grainy but real. Hair longer now. Belly swollen and round. She looked pale. Too thin. But she was alive. And his baby…

"Ivy," he whispered, fingers brushing the screen. "Look at her. She's so big now."

Mason stepped closer, his voice quiet. "You alright, man?"

"No," Lucas said, his voice rough. "I'm not. Not until she's in my arms again. Not until *he's dead.*"

He turned to the crew.

"Load every weapon. Every vest. Every knife. We're going in. And we're not coming out without them."

Lucas's hands shook as he strapped on his vest, locking the buckles with white-knuckled precision. He hadn't eaten in days, hadn't slept longer than an hour at a time. Rage and adrenaline were the only things keeping him upright.

"She's eight months now," he muttered to no one in particular, checking the ammo in his Glock. "Eight fucking months. Ivy could come any minute."

Mason stood in the corner, triple-checking the blueprints they'd pulled from CrossTech's database. "You sure about the location?"

Lucas nodded. "That signal was too clean. One of Ethan's men slipped up. I've got eyes on a second compound. It's more remote, harder to trace. Exactly where I'd hide a stolen life."

He moved to the screen, replaying the frozen security footage again, the frame he couldn't stop staring at.

Amelia.

Visibly pregnant.

Sitting on a thin mattress, clutching her stomach, eyes blank but somehow still defiant.

"She's trying to survive," Lucas said, voice rough. "I see it in her face. She hasn't given up on me."

"She's waiting for you," Mason agreed. "So we get her the hell out."

Lucas slammed his fist into the table, the screen flickering with the force. "I want every one of Ethan's men dead. I don't care if they drop their guns and beg. We show no mercy."

He turned to the crew, eyes bloodshot, grief and fury tangled like barbed wire in his chest.

"She's not just my girl. That's my *family* in there. My daughter. My entire fucking world."

Everyone nodded in silence.

Mason loaded the final round into his rifle and looked up. "What's the plan?"

Lucas stared at the map, then back at the grainy photo of

Amelia.

"We move in tonight," he said. "And we burn that place to the ground."

Forty-Five

Chapter 45

The pain came like a quiet knife. Sharp, sudden. Then gone.

Amelia froze on the cot, her hand instinctively going to her swollen belly.

Not yet. Please, not yet.

But another wave gripped her lower back, tighter this time. A pressure that stole her breath and made her legs tremble. She closed her eyes, counted slowly, tried to breathe through it like the books had said. The ones she'd been allowed. The ones that felt more like a cruel joke now.

When it passed, she blinked hard, her vision swimming. The concrete walls around her blurred like a fever dream. Ivy squirmed inside her like she was waking up, too. Like her tiny body already sensed the shift, the danger, the way Amelia's panic crackled like electricity under her skin.

"No," she whispered, cradling her bump with both hands. "Not yet, baby. Please stay with me a little longer."

Her heart thudded so hard it hurt. Sweat coated her hairline. She stood, or tried to gripping the edge of the rusted table beside the bed for balance.

Another pain hit, deeper now. Her knees buckled. She bit down on a scream.

"Ivy," she gasped, voice cracking. "Sweetheart, we have to hold on. We have to wait for Daddy. He's coming, I know he is."

The room spun, her body trembling as she paced in a tight circle, one hand gripping the curve of her stomach, the other pressed to her lower back. Her breathing grew rapid. The walls felt like they were closing in.

She couldn't give birth here.

Not in this prison.

Not with Ethan waiting on the other side of the door.

Not like this.

She sank to her knees, tears spilling freely now, her forehead pressed against the cold concrete floor as she whispered over and over like a prayer:

"You're not alone, Ivy. I'm here. I'm here. I'm going to protect you. Daddy's coming. Just hold on for him. Please… just a little longer."

Her entire body trembled as the next contraction rolled through her and this one didn't let go so quickly.

The contraction tore through her, vicious and sharp. Amelia gritted her teeth and screamed before she could stop herself, the sound ragged and helpless. It echoed off the concrete walls like a warning shot.

The door slammed open.

Ethan.

He stalked into the room like a storm in human skin, his eyes glittering with something feral, lips pulled into a mockery of a smile. "What now, princess?" he drawled. "Having a meltdown, or is our little guest getting restless?"

Amelia clutched her belly, her breath coming in shallow gasps. "Just stay away from me."

Ethan's boots echoed as he crossed the room. "I heard you scream," he said, crouching in front of her, mock-concern curling his voice like poison. "Is our baby girl eager to make her debut?"

She recoiled. "Don't call her that."

He grinned. "You don't like me playing daddy? Shame. You're doing so well. Swollen. Miserable. Ripe."

Her stomach twisted again, not from pain this time, but revulsion.

He tilted his head, voice turning sharp. "I said scream if there was a problem. So now we check."

He turned and barked, "Doctor!"

The lock clicked again, and the older man entered, his face tight with unease. He carried his bag, glancing between them before Ethan stepped back. "She's in pain," Ethan said. "Do your job."

Amelia was still trembling as the doctor put on gloves and knelt beside her. She couldn't stop the tears that slid silently down her cheeks, or the way her body stiffened under his clinical touch. Her nails dug into the mattress. She didn't look at Ethan. Couldn't.

"Contractions are irregular," the doctor murmured. "She's not in active labor. But there's some bleeding, likely from stress. She needs to stay still. Calm."

Ethan turned toward her slowly, eyes narrowed. "Then

maybe she should stop screaming like a little bitch."

Amelia flinched.

The doctor looked at her one last time, something like sympathy in his gaze. Then he packed up and left, the door clicking locked behind him.

Alone, Amelia curled onto her side, hands trembling over her belly. "You're okay," she whispered to Ivy, lips brushing her skin like a promise. "You're okay. I've got you. Daddy's coming. Just… hold on."

Forty-Six

Chapter 46

Ethan lit a cigarette with shaking fingers.

The smoke curled like sin around his jaw, the taste of it bitter, acrid but it helped. Slightly. He stared out the cracked window of the new hideout, a crumbling farmhouse surrounded by overgrown brush and woods that swallowed light. It had held them safe so far.

But now?

Now the air felt tighter. Thinner.

She was going to give birth soon.

He flicked the ash off the edge of the porch and turned to the nearest m. A tall brute with a scar under one eye and a semi-automatic slung over his chest.

"Tell them to double the perimeter. Nobody gets within a mile without me knowing."

The man nodded.

"I want eyes on every side," Ethan snapped. "Every tree.

Every fence post. If you see anything move. A bird, a fucking rabbit you shoot it. We're not taking chances."

He turned slowly, watching as his men snapped to attention. Five. No, six on site tonight. Plus the doctor, the idiot. And the two who handled transport.

"She's nearly ready," Ethan muttered, mostly to himself. Then louder, "The baby comes, she'll scream. We don't want anyone hearing that, do we?"

The men all murmured, "No, sir."

A flicker of doubt danced behind his eyes.

Lucas.

The name alone made his blood boil.

That bastard was still out there. Still breathing. Still trying to play the hero.

But he was always one step behind. Always too late.

"You see him, Lucas Cross you kill him. You don't hesitate. You don't wait to ask me. You put him in the ground before he ever gets a chance to say her name."

One of the men hesitated, then said, "Boss… we heard something. CrossTech… there's talk he might be getting closer."

Ethan's eyes snapped toward him, sharp as a blade.

"Then bury this place in shadows. Set the dogs loose. And if he gets within breathing distance of my girl…" Ethan's grin stretched too wide, too manic. "I'll gut him myself and make her watch."

He tossed the cigarette into the dirt, crushing it beneath his heel.

"Now go. Lock it down. We're almost at the finish line."

* * *

The pain twisted low in her abdomen, sharp and raw, ripping her from whatever shallow sleep she'd managed to fall into. She gasped, one hand flying to her belly, the other clutching the edge of the mattress as her body seized with another wave.

Not again.

Not now.

She rolled to her side, fingers trembling as she rubbed the swell of her belly. Ivy shifted beneath her skin, slow and restless, like she felt it too.

"Ivy," Amelia whispered, her voice shaking. "Baby girl… just stay with me. Not yet. Please, not yet."

Another contraction hit, harder this time. Her back arched off the bed, a low, strangled cry escaping her lips. She bit her knuckle to keep from screaming. If she screamed, Ethan would come. If he came…

She didn't finish the thought.

Tears blurred her vision. She breathed fast, uneven, trying to remember what the doctor had told her. Breathe deep. Slow. Ride it out.

But this wasn't just physical pain.

It was panic.

Her thoughts spiraled. What if this was labor? What if something was wrong? What if she gave birth here, with him watching, grinning, calling Ivy his?

Her heart slammed in her chest, each beat louder than the last. She was soaked in sweat, her nightshirt sticking to her spine. She felt like she was drowning.

She pulled herself upright, bracing against the wall, her forehead pressed to the concrete. Her knees buckled beneath her, but she stayed upright. She had to.

"For Ivy," she whispered. "For Lucas."

The door creaked open, metal grinding against metal.

Amelia flinched, already knowing who it would be before the voice reached her.

"Well, well," Ethan drawled from the doorway, grinning like he hadn't just kept her locked in hell for the last few months. "Is it time already, little dove?"

She didn't answer. Couldn't. Her breath came in short, shallow bursts, and her body trembled with the tail end of another contraction.

Behind him, the doctor followed with his bag, silent as always. Dead-eyed.

Ethan's boots thudded across the floor as he approached the bed. "You're early," he said softly, almost teasing. "Can't even wait for Daddy, huh?"

Amelia recoiled, scooting as far back against the headboard as she could, but it didn't matter. He grabbed her ankles and dragged her down the mattress with ease, ignoring her kicking, her gasps of pain. He positioned her legs open, knees bent, holding her down by the thighs as the doctor snapped on gloves.

"Don't squirm," Ethan said, voice low. "You'll hurt the baby. And we wouldn't want that, now would we?"

"Don't touch me," Amelia hissed, tears streaming, her voice hoarse. "Please don't."

"Hush," he murmured. "Be still. Let the doctor do his work."

She sobbed as the doctor moved between her legs, cold hands pressing, prodding. She tried to look away, tried to think of Lucas, of Ivy's soft kicks, of anything but this moment.

But Ethan was still there, hovering above her like a predator, rubbing her thigh in mock comfort.

"She's dilated," the doctor muttered. "Four centimeters. Could be hours. Could be sooner."

Ethan smiled. "She's getting ready, then. Good. We'll need everything perfect when she arrives."

He leaned closer, his breath foul against her cheek.

"You're going to push her out right here, Amelia," he whispered, fingers stroking her stomach possessively. "And I'm going to be the first thing she sees."

She screamed and tried to kick him, but he pinned her knees tighter, smirking.

The doctor stood, unfazed. "She needs to rest between contractions. Keep her calm. Any stress could trigger a complication."

"She'll be fine," Ethan said smoothly, releasing her at last. "Won't you, dove?"

Amelia curled onto her side the second he stepped back, arms wrapped tight around her belly.

She didn't speak.

Didn't cry.

But inside, her soul screamed.

She needed Lucas.

She needed him now.

Forty-Seven

Chapter 47

They moved like shadows, silent, surgical, lethal.

Lucas didn't breathe right. Couldn't. Not when he knew she was in there. Somewhere inside that concrete hell, pregnant and alone. He'd seen the feed. Her belly was so big now it looked like it hurt to carry. Eight months. Eight fucking months. And he hadn't been there.

That thought burned more than anything.

He was at the front. Of course he was. No one else was getting to her first.

"Two guards by the west entrance," Jax whispered from behind. "Camera sweep every thirty seconds."

Lucas didn't answer. He was already moving.

The knife in his hand wasn't for show. It kissed the side of the first guard's throat like a lover and slid deep, silencing the man with a gurgle. Lucas caught him before he hit the ground.

No hesitation. No remorse.

The second went down just as fast. A boot to the knee, a fist to the throat, and a blade to finish. Lucas's grip was steady. Cold. Focused.

Every body that dropped was one step closer to Amelia.

He'd stormed safe houses. Bled snitches dry for leads. Hacked into systems that would've made his lawyers cry. None of it mattered until now. Until he was here.

Inside.

Mason slid in behind him, gun raised. "Still with me?"

Lucas didn't look. "We don't stop until I'm holding her."

They moved room by room, clearing it with ghost-quiet steps and blood-slick efficiency. One guard tried to run. Lucas caught him, slammed him into the wall, and drove his blade into the gut with a twisted snarl.

"You work for Ethan?" he hissed. "You help him touch her?"

The man gurgled something pathetic. Lucas didn't wait. He drove the blade up through the ribs, twisted, and let him drop.

"I'll kill every single one of you before I let him touch her again."

He wiped the blade on the man's shirt and kept moving. Jax and Mason flanked him. His entire crew had gone feral. Masks on, eyes hard, weapons ready. They knew what this meant to him.

What it meant to her.

They reached a locked hallway, security-grade door. Mason tapped into the control panel, fingers flying.

"Give me ten seconds," he muttered.

Lucas's fist slammed into the wall beside him. "Give me five."

The door clicked. Lucas was already pushing through.

Then he saw it, a flickering feed on the tablet Mason held

out to him.

Amelia.

She was there, center frame, bathed in that same dim yellow light, sweat clinging to her skin like a second layer. Her hair was matted, her shirt soaked through at the chest and belly. Her hands clutched the sides of a stained mattress, knuckles white with pressure, body curled forward like she was trying to survive a storm from the inside out.

Then she screamed.

A sound so raw it nearly brought him to his knees.

"She's in labor," he whispered. "She's... she's having Ivy."

Mason sucked in a breath. "Shit."

"No," Lucas growled. His voice broke, catching against something sharp in his chest. "No, no, not without me. She can't...she can't do this without me."

He pressed closer to the screen, like somehow being closer to the feed meant he could reach through it. Touch her. Tell her to hold on.

Amelia screamed again, and this time he caught it, a whisper between her cries.

"Lucas... please..."

His heart shattered.

He clenched his jaw so hard his teeth ached, fists trembling as he watched her writhe on that fucking mattress like an animal caught in a trap. Alone. In pain. Carrying the child they made together in love, while surrounded by monsters who would never deserve to breathe the same air as her.

"She's begging for me," he whispered.

The next words came out low. Vicious.

"I'm going to burn this place to the ground."

He didn't look at Mason, didn't need to. His eyes were

locked on the screen as Amelia gasped, her hand gripping her belly like she was holding their daughter in.

"She's not going to die in that room," he said. "And our daughter is not taking her first breath surrounded by these fucking animals."

Mason nodded once. "Then we move."

Lucas stepped back, sliding the tablet into his vest.

"Gear up," he growled. "We go now. No sound. No mercy. Anyone standing between me and that room dies."

He paused, looking back at the screen for just one more second, her face twisted in pain, her mouth open on another cry.

"Hold on, baby," he whispered. "Daddy's coming."

* * *

The message reached him before dawn.

Cross hit another site. Nine dead. No survivors.

And still no Amelia.

Ethan laughed, low, breathless, unhinged until it turned into something like a snarl. "He's not chasing me," he muttered, grabbing his coat. "He's chasing a ghost."

He shoved the door to her room open so hard it banged against the wall.

The light inside was sterile, harsh. The air thick with bleach and fear.

Amelia was there. Pale, sweating, gripping the edge of the bed so tightly her knuckles blanched. The thin sheet beneath her was damp, and her breath came in broken sobs. Another contraction tore through her, bending her in half with a sound that wasn't quite human.

"Lucas…" she gasped. "Please…"

Ethan smiled like the sound of her pain was music. "He can't hear you, sweetheart. But I can."

He turned to the doctor who stood frozen in the corner. "Well?"

The old man swallowed hard, hands shaking. "She's progressing fast. The contractions are less than three minutes apart. We're close."

Ethan stepped forward, boots echoing on the concrete. "How close?"

"Eight, maybe nine centimeters."

Ethan's tongue pressed against the inside of his cheek. He stared down at Amelia, at the tremor in her hands, at the way she shielded her belly like she could hide what was his. "Good," he said finally. "We've waited long enough."

Another contraction hit. Amelia bit back a scream, eyes rolling as she breathed through it. Ethan crouched beside her bed, his voice calm, too calm. "You feel that?" he asked quietly. "That's what happens when you fight me. Every time you try to run, your body remembers who it answers to."

"Go to hell," she spat, shaking with pain.

He chuckled. "Hell? You're already there. You've been here since the day you left me."

The doctor fumbled with his tools, trying to steady his hands. Amelia's breath came sharp, panicked. Ethan leaned closer, brushing a lock of damp hair from her face with the back of his knuckle. "You were supposed to make me rich, Amelia. You and your pretty little screams. But you ran. You stole from me."

He leaned in until she could feel the heat of his breath. "So now I'm taking everything back. You'll give me this baby, and you'll learn what it means to be truly owned."

Amelia's body shook with another contraction. She gripped the mattress so tightly the seams split under her nails. "You'll never touch her," she rasped.

Ethan smiled. "You said the same thing once, remember? About yourself."

He turned to the doctor, his tone cutting through the air like a blade. "Keep her alive. If she bleeds too much, you bleed more. If the baby dies, so do you."

The doctor nodded rapidly, terrified. "Yes, Mr. Walker."

Ethan straightened, adjusting his jacket. Before he left, he paused by the door, looking back at her. "When she's born, Amelia, I want you to look at me first. You hear? Because I'll be the first thing she ever sees."

The door slammed. The sound echoed long after he was gone.

Amelia curled on her side, hands trembling over her stomach. She whispered to the life inside her, desperate, voice cracking.

"Ivy, it's almost over. Just a little longer, my love. Daddy's coming. He's coming, I swear."

Her whole body trembled as another contraction built, her mind fraying between pain and fear and love. She bit down hard on her lip to stop from screaming, whispering through her tears.

"I'll do anything to keep you safe."

Forty-Eight

Chapter 48

Amelia's scream cracked the silence.

It wasn't just pain anymore.

It was fear. Pressure. A deep, primal ache ripping her from the inside out.

"Ten centimeters," the doctor muttered. "She's ready. It's time."

She could barely focus. Sweat clung to her skin, her hands gripping the edge of the bed so tight her knuckles had gone white.

Then the sound came, *a door slamming.* Heavy boots. A thud. A *gunshot.*

And then—*his voice.*

"Amelia!"

Her head snapped toward the sound, tears already springing to her eyes.

"Lucas?" Her voice was hoarse, barely above a whisper.

"Lucas!"

The door burst open like the climax of a nightmare finally breaking.

And there he was.

Bloodied. Breathing hard. Eyes on *fire*.

Lucas took one look at her, legs spread, belly taut and trembling, Ethan standing too fucking close and saw red.

"Get. Away. From her," he growled.

Ethan laughed, stepping back just a fraction, arms spread like he was welcoming death. "Too late, lover boy. She's already mine."

Lucas didn't wait.

He charged.

The two collided rage and obsession locked in a brutal dance. Fists flew.

Amelia screamed, trying to sit up, her body torn between labor and terror.

He landed punch after punch, blood splattering his shirt. "You kept her from me," he snarled. "You touched her. You made her scream, I'll fucking end you."

Ethan's grin was stained red. "And you're too late."

Then the knife came out.

A flash of silver.

A cry.

Lucas gasped, stumbling, blood soaking through his side.

"NO!" Amelia's voice cracked. *"Lucas!"*

Ethan turned, gloating. "Oops."

Amelia's eyes flicked to the floor, Lucas's gun lay discarded in the chaos.

She didn't think.

She *moved*.

With a grunt of pain and pure fury, she rolled to the edge of the bed, reached down, grabbed the gun, and aimed it straight at Ethan.

"Get away from him," she snarled, finger tightening on the trigger.

Ethan turned, laughing…

Bang.

One shot.

Right between the eyes.

He dropped like a puppet with its strings cut.

Silence.

Her chest heaved. Her arms shook. She dropped the gun and crawled to Lucas, her contractions still ripping through her as tears poured down her cheeks.

Amelia screamed—raw, torn, primal.

Her body buckled under the force of another contraction. Her fingers trembled as she reached for Lucas, who still wasn't moving.

"Lucas… please," she sobbed. Her hands cupped his bloodied face. "You found me. You got to me. You don't get to die now."

Mason was on the floor beside him, one hand pressed hard to Lucas's wound, soaked in blood. "He's losing a lot," he muttered. "Too much."

Amelia's legs spread instinctively as the next wave of pressure hit. Her whole body clenched with pain.

"I…I can feel her coming," she gasped, voice cracking. "Mason, I…I think I'm pushing."

Mason turned sharply. "Shit. Okay. Okay…fuck." He looked down at Lucas, then back at her. "I need to stop the bleeding. I can't leave him, Amelia."

"Then don't!" she cried. "Just…talk me through it. Call for medics. Please."

Mason didn't hesitate. He reached for the radio clipped to his belt with one bloodied hand.

"Dispatch. We need a medic team, *now*. Female in active labor. Male with a stab wound. Critical. GPS locked."

He dropped the radio. "They're en route."

Another contraction tore through Amelia's spine. She screamed again, collapsing forward onto her hands and knees. "Oh God…I can't..I can't…it hurts so much!"

"You're strong," Mason said fiercely. "You made it this far. You're right there, Amelia. You just need to breathe."

Amelia whimpered, looking at Lucas. "She needs you," she whispered. "I need you."

Her voice broke. "Please wake up, Lucas. Please…please, I can't do this alone again."

She shifted, propping herself against the wall, legs open, body trembling. "I can feel her…she's so low…oh God….*she's coming!*"

Mason kept his hand firm on Lucas's wound, glancing over. "She's crowning. Amelia…one more push. Just one."

"I love you," she whispered to Lucas. "Come back to me. Come back to *her.*"

She screamed…long, loud, and broken as she pushed.

And then…

A cry. Wet. Sharp. Beautiful.

The sound shattered the air like sunlight.

Mason's chest heaved. "She's here."

Lucas stirred.

A choked breath left his lips as his eyes cracked open.

"Ivy…?" he rasped.

Amelia sobbed. "Yes. Yes…she's here."

She pulled the tiny baby to her chest, skin-to-skin, tears falling onto Ivy's cheeks. "We did it. Lucas, we…we have her."

Lucas's bloody hand reached out, trembling. "Let me…see her…"

Mason grabbed more gauze, pressing tighter to his side. "Stay still, man. Help's almost here. Just keep looking at your girls."

Amelia pressed her face to Ivy's head. "We're okay now," she whispered, her voice shaking. "You're safe. We're safe."

And outside, the sound of sirens began to rise.

Red lights flashed against the walls.

Boots thundered down the corridor. The smell of gunpowder and blood clung to everything.

Medics burst into the room, ducking under Mason's arm to reach Lucas.

"Pulse weak but steady," one of them called. "Get pressure on that wound, keep him conscious."

Mason didn't move his hand from Lucas's side. His voice was rough. "He's lost a lot. You're gonna need fluids *now*."

"Copy that." Tubes and gauze scattered across the floor. They worked fast, methodical. Lucas's chest lifted in shallow, broken breaths.

Amelia watched from where she lay, Ivy bundled against her chest. Her body trembled. Her skin was pale and slick with sweat.

She smiled weakly through the haze. "See, Ivy? Daddy's okay… Daddy's going to be okay…"

But the edges of her vision started to blur.

One of the medics turned. "She's bleeding. Someone get over here!"

Amelia looked down. The sheet beneath her was dark with blood. Too much. It spread fast.

"No—no, no, no…" she whispered, shaking her head. "I can't…please, I can't…"

Lucas stirred at the sound of her voice. "Amelia?" His tone was rough, broken. His gaze found her and froze. "Why's there…why's there so much blood?"

"She's hemorrhaging!" the medic shouted. "I need clamps and fluids, *now!*"

Mason pressed a blood-soaked towel harder to Lucas's side. "Don't you move," he ordered, voice shaking. "You stay right here."

Lucas tried to push up anyway, his hand slipping in the blood between them. "Help her! *Help her!*"

Amelia's head lolled. Her voice was faint, fragile. "Lucas… don't… don't let go…"

He reached for her, desperate, his eyes wild. "You hold on, baby. You hear me? *You hold on for Ivy.*"

Her fingers brushed his before slipping away.

"Her pulse is dropping!" a medic yelled. "We're losing her!"

"Don't you fucking say that!" Lucas roared, his voice cracking in half. "You save her! You save both of them!"

The medic injected something into Amelia's IV, another pressing down on her abdomen. "We've got her. Stay with us, Amelia, stay with us."

Lucas's breath hitched. He stared helplessly across the space between them. His world bleeding out on the floor.

"Come on, baby," he whispered, his voice breaking completely. "You made it through hell. Don't stop now. Don't you dare stop now."

Ivy let out a small cry , the sound cutting through the chaos.

And somewhere, in that sound, Amelia's chest rose again, barely, but enough. The monitor beeped once, then steady again.

Mason exhaled, trembling. "She's still with us."

Lucas slumped back, tears streaking down his face. "Don't ever do that again," he whispered. "You don't get to leave me. Not now. Not ever."

The compound pulsed with the red strobe of emergency lights now, flashing over blood-slick floors and fallen bodies. The medics worked quickly, efficiently, adrenaline burning through the air like acid.

One stretcher held Lucas, barely conscious and weak, his chest rising in shallow, ragged breaths beneath the blood-soaked gauze. His head lolled to the side as they lifted him, but his eyes fluttered, fighting to stay awake.

"I'm going with him," Mason said firmly, Ivy cradled against his chest in a white blanket that was far too clean for this place.

"You're not family," one medic argued.

"I'm all she's got right now," Mason growled, his voice ice. "You want me to hand this baby to a stranger? Not fucking happening."

They didn't argue again. He climbed into the ambulance beside Lucas. Ivy fussed in his arms, her cry high and uncertain.

Mason looked down at her. So small. So alive.

"Hey," he whispered, brushing her cheek with one thick thumb. "You're tough like your mama, huh? And your dad...

he's a stubborn bastard. He's not leaving you either."

His hands trembled around her tiny, swaddled body. Her skin was warm, so impossibly soft, and her little face scrunched up every time the siren wailed too close. Mason leaned over, his hands gentle for once as he pressed the tiny, bundled form into Lucas's arms. "She needs her dad now," he said gruffly, voice rough with relief. Lucas blinked hard, cradling Ivy close, the warmth of her life trembling in his hands, anchoring him to the world again.

"They're taking Amelia to the trauma ward. Too much blood loss. She's unconscious."

Lucas flinched like the words hit bone. "What?" His voice cracked. "She was talking. She…she held my hand."

"She passed out just before they loaded her. The medics are doing everything they can."

Lucas looked down at Ivy, then pressed his forehead to hers. "You hold on, baby girl. And she will too. She has to."

Ivy made a soft sound, like a hiccup mixed with a sob and Lucas lost it.

"I should've been there." His voice broke. "All those months. I should've…fuck, I should've burned the world down sooner."

Mason stayed quiet, just watching him hold his daughter.

"I saw her on that fucking screen screaming in labor," Lucas whispered. "And I wasn't there. I didn't catch her when she fell. I didn't… I didn't get to tell her it was okay."

"You're here now," Mason said. "You saved her."

"No." Lucas shook his head slowly. "She saved us. She shot that bastard herself. Crawled across the room, gave birth. Amelia is the strongest person I've ever known."

The ambulance hit a bump and Ivy whimpered. Lucas instantly rocked her, pressing her close.

"Shh, shh… Daddy's got you," he murmured, lips brushing the crown of her head. "Daddy's right here."

He looked to Mason, voice barely steady. "Call the hospital again. I need to know the second she wakes up."

"I already did," Mason said quietly. "You'll be the first to know."

Lucas looked back down at Ivy. This perfect little soul that bore none of the world's horrors yet. And he knew, in that moment, there was nothing he wouldn't do to keep her and Amelia safe now.

Nothing.

Forty-Nine

Chapter 49

The hallway smelled like antiseptic and blood and something sharp he couldn't name. Lucas sat hunched on the edge of the gurney, one hand clutching the stained edge of his shirt, the other curled into a fist that wouldn't stop shaking.

He kept hearing Ivy's cry in his head.

Her first breath. The way her little mouth had opened wide like she was already fighting to live.

She was everything.

And so was Amelia.

A nurse returned, cradling Ivy in her arms, swaddled tight in a hospital blanket. Mason was close behind, hovering like a fucking hawk.

"She's perfect," the nurse said, gently placing Ivy into Mason's arms. "We're going to do a full check-up now. Just precautionary."

Lucas's eyes locked on his daughter.

"Mason," he said, voice rough. "Go with her. Don't let her out of your sight."

Mason nodded immediately and turned with her, his shoulders squaring like he was ready to throw punches in the pediatric ward if he had to.

As soon as they disappeared down the hall, Lucas turned to the nearest doctor. "Where's Amelia? Tell me she's okay."

The doctor hesitated, flipping through a chart. That moment of silence was a blade against Lucas's throat.

"She lost a significant amount of blood," the doctor finally said. "We rushed her into surgery to stop the hemorrhaging. The team's doing everything they can."

"Is she…?" Lucas couldn't finish the sentence. Couldn't let his mouth form the words.

"She's alive. For now. But it's serious."

Lucas felt the hospital tilt sideways.

His stitches burned, but he didn't flinch. A nurse gently sat him back down, starting to suture his wound. He barely noticed the needle.

All he could see was her face.

All he could hear was her voice, that final scream as Ivy came into the world.

And now silence.

"She's going to be okay," he whispered to himself. "She's strong. She's the strongest person I know."

The nurse gave him a small look. "She has you. That counts for something."

He didn't answer. Just stared at the hallway where they'd taken her.

"Come back to me, Amelia," he whispered. "You don't get to leave me. Not now. Not after we made it."

Lucas looked up.

Mason had his daughter.

Wrapped in a hospital blanket too big for her small body, Ivy was nestled against Mason's chest like something sacred. Her little hand peeked out, fingers curled into a tight fist. Like she was already ready to fight.

Lucas exhaled a breath he hadn't realized he'd been holding.

"She's okay," Mason said, voice low, reverent. "Strong. Healthy lungs on her, too. Screamed the whole time they checked her over. Didn't stop until they swaddled her."

Lucas tried to stand, but his side pulled hard, stitches still fresh. He winced, growling under his breath.

Mason crossed the space, stepping close and slowly, carefully, transferred the bundle into Lucas's waiting arms.

The world stopped.

She was so small.

So unbelievably small.

Lucas stared down at her, heart stuttering. Her lashes were dark and fluttery, her mouth shaped like a rosebud. His thumb brushed along the edge of her cheek. She made a soft noise, something like a sigh, and settled against him like she knew him.

Like she *felt* him.

Lucas swallowed the lump that threatened to shatter him completely.

"Hi, baby girl," he whispered. "It's Daddy."

Mason stood nearby, arms crossed, watching the moment like it mattered to him too.

Lucas leaned down, pressed his lips to Ivy's forehead. "Your mum's going to be okay," he murmured. "She has to be."

As if on cue, a nurse entered.

"She's out of surgery," the nurse said. "Still critical, but stable. She's being moved to recovery."

Lucas's head jerked up. "Can I see her?"

"Soon. We just need a bit more time."

He nodded, but the fire behind his eyes reignited.

"She fought like hell," he told the nurse. "You better fight just as hard for her."

The nurse gave him a soft smile. "She's in good hands."

Lucas looked down at Ivy again, tears burning behind his eyes.

"You're going to meet your mum soon, little one," he whispered. "And when you do, you tell her I never stopped looking."

Chapter 50

The beeping of machines was steady. Too steady.

Too quiet for the storm still living in Lucas's chest.

Amelia lay on the hospital bed, pale, still, her eyes closed. The bruises on her arms had faded to yellow, but the damage went deeper. A machines beeped beside her, tubes in her arms. Her hair, dark and matted with sweat, clung to her temple. She looked so damn fragile. And so goddamn beautiful.

Lucas sat beside her, one arm cradling Ivy against his chest. The baby was wrapped snugly in a soft pink hospital blanket, her tiny face nestled against his chest. Her breathing was shallow but steady. She smelled like powder and something he couldn't name. Something pure.

Mason stood a few steps away, arms crossed, eyes locked on Amelia like he might will her to wake up.

A nurse stepped in quietly, clipboard in hand.

"She's stable," she whispered. "Lost a lot of blood, but the surgery went well. She's fighting."

Lucas nodded, jaw tight.

"She always does."

The nurse gave a gentle smile and left the room again.

Lucas turned back to Amelia. He leaned in, brushing her hair from her forehead with shaking fingers.

"I need you to wake up, baby," he whispered, voice hoarse. "You did it. She's here. You kept her safe."

He adjusted Ivy in his arms and leaned forward so Amelia could feel them both close. "She has your mouth. Your little chin. She's already so stubborn."

Mason chuckled under his breath.

Lucas glanced back at him, voice cracking. "I don't know how to do this without her."

"You're not going to have to," Mason said softly. "She's coming back. Just give her a minute."

Lucas swallowed hard and turned back to Amelia, resting Ivy gently beside her on the bed, nestled in the crook of her mother's arm.

"Come on, baby," he whispered. "Come back to us."

A long moment passed. Then…

Her fingers twitched.

Lucas sat up straight. "Amelia?"

Another twitch. Then her lashes fluttered.

"Lucas?" Her voice was broken and dry, barely audible.

He surged forward, eyes shining. "I'm here. I've got you."

Her eyes blinked open, glassy and confused. "The baby?"

"She's perfect." Lucas lifted Ivy, holding her so Amelia could see. "You did it, baby. She's perfect."

Tears slid down Amelia's cheeks. Her hand reached, trembling, toward Ivy. Lucas helped guide her fingers to the baby's cheek.

"Ivy," she whispered. "I want to name her Ivy Rose."

Lucas leaned forward and pressed his forehead to hers. "Then Ivy Rose it is."

She let out a quiet sob. "You found me."

"Always," he breathed, brushing a kiss to her temple. "I'll always find you."

Mason cleared his throat quietly and turned toward the window, giving them a moment.

But Lucas didn't move.

He just held her. Held them both. His whole world finally back in his arms.

The room was quiet now. Peaceful in a way Amelia hadn't felt in months.

Soft moonlight spilled through the blinds, casting pale lines across the sterile floor. The machines still beeped, but slower now, less urgent, more like a lullaby.

Amelia lay propped in the hospital bed, an IV still in her arm, her skin pale but warm. Her eyes were tired but alive. She was clean. Bandaged. Safe. And in her arms, wrapped in a fresh blanket, was Ivy Rose.

Lucas sat beside her, one hand protectively on her thigh, the other gently cupping the baby's tiny back. He hadn't let go of either of them since they wheeled her into this room hours ago.

"I still can't believe she's real," Amelia whispered, voice husky from exhaustion. She looked down at Ivy, the baby's little lips parting in her sleep. "I didn't think I'd make it."

Lucas kissed her shoulder, his lips lingering. "But you did. You fought like hell, and you brought our girl into the world."

Tears stung her eyes, but she didn't wipe them. Let them fall. She'd earned every one.

There was a quiet knock at the door before Mason stepped in. He looked awkward for once, his normally hard gaze softened, arms folded but not defensive.

He took a step closer. "How're you feeling?"

Amelia smiled tiredly. "Like I've been hit by a truck. Twice."

He huffed a soft laugh and moved to the side of the bed. He didn't say anything at first, just looked at her. Like he was checking to make sure this wasn't another hallucination. That she was really here.

Then, gently, he leaned down and kissed her forehead.

"I'm glad you're okay," he murmured.

Her eyes filled again, and she reached out to squeeze his hand. "You kept Lucas safe. Thank you."

Mason's jaw flexed, but he nodded. "Always."

He glanced at the baby, who let out a tiny noise in her sleep, and then looked back at them both with something unspoken in his eyes. Respect. Loyalty. Love in his own quiet, guarded way.

"I'll be right outside," he said, backing toward the door. "No one's getting in. Not tonight."

Lucas nodded his thanks as Mason stepped out, quietly pulling the door shut behind him.

And then it was just them.

Their little family.

Lucas shifted closer on the bed, resting his forehead to Amelia's as they stared down at their daughter.

"We're okay," he whispered.

Amelia let out a shaky breath and finally, finally let herself believe it.

"Yeah," she whispered back. "We're really okay."

Fifty-One

Chapter 51

Two Days Later. Hospital Discharge

The sky was blue. Soft. Like it had been waiting for this moment too.

Lucas stood just outside the hospital entrance, one hand resting protectively on Amelia's lower back as she stepped slowly toward the waiting car. She moved slowly, wrapped in a loose black cardigan, her body still healing, but she held Ivy close to her chest, the baby's head tucked beneath her chin.

Mason stood by the car, opening the door. He'd been quiet all morning, but efficient as always. He'd picked up the custom-fitted car seat, brought a blanket, even stocked the fridge at the house without being asked.

Lucas nodded to him. "Thanks for getting the place ready."

Mason grunted. "Didn't want your girls coming home to chaos."

He helped Amelia into the car, "You're safe now," he murmured

The drive home was silent, sacred.

Lucas watched Amelia in the rear view mirror as she dozed lightly, Ivy sleeping in her car seat. He reached back, resting his fingers lightly on her knee. She opened her eyes at the touch and gave him a soft, tired smile.

Home.

The house was warm. Clean. Dimly lit by soft lamps Mason had left on. The scent of fresh sheets and baby powder lingered in the air.

Lucas helped Amelia into bed, placing Ivy in the bassinet beside her. She winced a little as she lay back, but her eyes never left him.

"I didn't think we'd make it here," she whispered.

Lucas sat beside her, stroking a hand through her hair. "Neither did I."

She reached for his hand, lacing their fingers. "But we did."

He leaned in and kissed her, soft and slow, careful not to push her healing body too hard. But the emotion in it wrecked them both. His breath shuddered when he pulled away.

"I want it all with you, Amelia," he said. "Marriage. A backyard for Ivy. Maybe a dog. I don't care what it looks like. I just want you. Our family. Peace."

Her eyes welled with tears. "You really think we'll get peace?"

He nodded. "We've fought through hell to earn it."

She pressed her forehead to his. "Then let's build it."

They sat like that for a long time, her hand on his thigh, his wrapped around hers. Ivy stirred in the bassinet, a tiny whimper escaping her lips before she settled again.

Their home was no longer just bricks and walls.

It was built from blood, from fire, from love.

Steam rose in lazy curls from the shallow baby bath as Lucas knelt beside the tub, shirt sleeves rolled up, one hand supporting Ivy's fragile neck. She was only days old, and yet, to him, she was already everything.

Amelia sat close on a stool, still moving slow from recovery, watching her two loves with a smile so full it could crack the world open.

"She's so tiny," Lucas whispered, awe softening every edge of his voice. "Like… impossibly small."

"She was inside me three days ago," Amelia replied, tired but glowing. "Now look at her."

Ivy squeaked as the warm water lapped against her belly, her legs kicking lightly. Lucas dipped a soft cloth into the bath and ran it gently along her arm, his hands reverent, careful.

"She's strong already. Just like her mum." His gaze lifted to Amelia's. "You were… fuck, Amelia. You were a warrior."

She swallowed hard, eyes misting. "I was so scared. I thought I was going to die."

"But you didn't." He cupped Ivy's head, leaned in to press a kiss to her damp crown. "You fought. For her. For us."

Amelia's voice cracked. "I didn't want her to be born without you."

Lucas looked up, meeting her eyes with the kind of love that felt ancient. "And now she never has to be."

When the bath was done and Ivy was bundled in a hooded bunny towel, Amelia took her in her arms. Lucas cleaned up in silence, his jaw tight, his mind somewhere deeper.

She watched him. The tension in his shoulders. The way he moved like he still expected to fight someone.

She was about to ask what was wrong, when he turned and walked straight to her dropping to one knee.

Lucas looked up at her from the floor of their bedroom, kneeling like it was sacred. His hands shook slightly, and he held something small and black in one palm.

"I didn't plan this," he said. "Didn't have a speech. Hell, I didn't even know if I'd live long enough to get this moment."

Amelia's breath caught. Her arms tightened around Ivy.

"But then I watched you give birth to our daughter. I watched you survive the darkest shit anyone could live through. And all I could think about, while you were screaming, while you were bleeding, while I was begging the universe not to take you from me was this."

He opened the box. A ring sat inside. Simple. Silver. Timeless.

"I want to grow old with you. I want to build a life that doesn't hurt. I want to wake up every morning and know you're still mine. That she's safe. That we made it."

Tears streamed down Amelia's cheeks.

"So I'm asking you, not because we've been through hell, but because we deserve heaven. Will you marry me, Amelia?"

She choked out a laugh, holding Ivy close to her chest.

"Yes," she whispered, then louder, "Yes, Lucas."

He stood, kissed her like it was the first time all over again, and pressed his forehead to hers.

Their baby girl stirred in her arms, eyes fluttering open just long enough to blink up at them, like she already knew.

The world didn't feel dangerous anymore.

It felt like home.

Epilogue

Three Months Later. Their Wedding Day

The garden had never looked more alive.

Soft white fabric drifted in the breeze, tied to wooden archways that lined the backyard. Wildflowers spilled over tables and trellises, sun-warmed and honey-sweet. The late spring air smelled like lavender, fresh grass, and something new, something whole.

Amelia stood barefoot on the back porch, her dress light and flowing, ivory lace brushing her ankles. Her hair was twisted up with little white roses, loose strands falling around her face. Ivy gurgled on her hip, three months old now, cheeks round and rosy, a tiny crown of baby's breath nestled into her soft brown curls.

"She's grown so much," Mason said from the doorway, dressed in a crisp black shirt, sleeves rolled to the elbows. "Looks just like you."

Amelia smiled, eyes never leaving the view of the archway where Lucas waited.

"He's been pacing for the last twenty minutes," Mason added with a smirk. "Said if he didn't see you soon, he was marching in here and marrying you in the kitchen."

She laughed softly. "That sounds like him."

Mason stepped closer and kissed Ivy's head. "I'll walk you down, if you want."

"I'd like that."

As they stepped out, the crowd quieted. Only a small gathering, just the people who mattered. The crew. Everyone who had bled for them, fought for them. Some of the old CrossTech team, too, smiling through watery eyes. They'd all seen what Lucas and Amelia had survived. Today was about what came after.

Lucas stood under the arch, black dress shirt open at the collar, sleeves rolled, tattoos showing. His eyes were locked on her, and when he saw Ivy in her arms, he swore under his breath and smiled like he might cry.

"You look like a dream," he whispered when she reached him.

Amelia passed Ivy gently to Mason, who held her like she was made of starlight.

"You ready for forever?" she asked, voice shaking.

Lucas reached for her hands, threading their fingers together. "Baby, I've been ready since the moment I saw you in the coffee shop."

The vows were short, real. Spoken like promises etched into bone.

"I will never leave you in the dark again," Lucas said, voice thick. "I will protect you, love you, raise our daughter with you… until I take my last breath."

Amelia wiped a tear from his cheek and whispered, "You already gave me everything, Lucas. This… this is just us starting over. With peace."

"You may kiss the bride," Mason called out from beside them, rocking Ivy gently.

Lucas didn't wait.

The kiss wasn't rushed, but it was deep, full of everything they'd been through. Ivy squealed at the sound of cheering and Mason lifted her into the air with a quiet laugh.

They danced under the string lights that night, barefoot in the grass.

Lucas held Amelia close, his hand on the small of her back, her head tucked under his chin. Ivy napped nearby in a wicker bassinet lined with wildflowers, watched over by Mason and Jax, who refused to let anyone near without clearance.

It was safe here.

It was home.

And for the first time in years, Amelia could breathe.

Afterword

To every single reader who's made it to this point thank you.

From the bottom of my heart, thank you for going on this journey with Amelia and Lucas.

This story was never meant to be an easy one. It was messy. Raw. Haunting. Full of pain, but also full of love that refused to die.

I knew from the beginning that Amelia's story would test limits. That Lucas would break and rebuild. That trauma would leave scars but healing would find them anyway, slowly, stubbornly, beautifully.

Writing this book took pieces of me. But it also gave something back. It reminded me of the strength in survival, the softness in choosing to love again, and the fire that still burns in the darkest of places.

If you cried with them, fought beside them, screamed at the pages, I see you.

If you've ever been shattered and still found a way to breathe again, this story was for you.

And if you're holding onto hope, like Amelia once did, just know:

Love doesn't have to be perfect to be powerful.
Sometimes, it just has to survive.
Until next time
With all my heart,
Chantel Nunn

www.ingramcontent.com/pod-product-compliance
Lightning Source LLC
Chambersburg PA
CBHW061527210726
48287CB00006B/1863